Forever Classics

GOLDEN GATES

Jean Conrad

is an imprint of
Guideposts Associates, Inc.
Carmel, NY 10512

A Note from the Author:
I love to hear from my readers! You may correspond with me by writing:

Jean Conrad
Author Relations
1415 Lake Drive, S.E.
Grand Rapids, MI 49506

This Guideposts edition is published by special arrangement with Zondervan Publishing House.

Scripture quotations are taken from the King James Version of the Bible.

Edited by Nancye Willis
Designed by Kim Koning

Printed in the United States of America

For my husband, Joseph, whose life and ideals provide a model for the true Christian hero

CHAPTER 1

A STIFF WIND FILLED square-rigged sails as the *Yankee Clipper* swept grandly through the strait known as the Golden Gate into San Francisco Bay. The year was 1855, and the ship had just completed a voyage from New York in a record eighty-nine days. Only a few years before, the swift passage would have been greeted with cheers by passengers eager to strike it rich in the gold fields at Sutter's Mill on the American River. Now the gold rush of 1849 was over, and the sea-weary merchants, settlers, and bankers who crowded the *Yankee Clipper*'s deck rejoiced more quietly, to match their more moderate expectations.

Nonetheless, the fabled entrance to California's bonanzas had not lost all its magic. California's glorious sunshine turned sand dunes on each side of the passage a deep yellow, caused the waves to shine, and washed the Golden Gate in a promise of opportunity and adventure.

Leaning against the ship's railing, Marianna Windemere sensed an undercurrent of excitement and frowned. She had no intention of catching the western fever. Two years earlier her sister Gloriana had taken this same voyage on her way to becoming a missionary nurse in Oregon Territory. Gloriana had married a westerner and settled down in a remote village called Applegate Landing.

"I'm not going to bury myself in the wilderness," Marianna told herself firmly, giving her head a decided shake and setting the glossy brown curls bouncing around her fashionable, if unattractive, coal scuttle bonnet. At twenty-two Marianna was unmistakably lovely and just as unmistakably unhappy. The severe fashions that failed to flatter most women only emphasized her beauty. The wide hoop skirts called attention to the smallness of her waist, and the short, layered cape set off her graceful shoulders. Her hair—parted in the middle and falling in luxurious curls around her ears and neck—framed a face set with enormous blue eyes fringed by long, curling lashes. Her cheeks were only a shade lighter than her vibrantly pink, full mouth, now drooping slightly at the corners. Her expression suggested not only discontent but distrust and distaste as she waited for her first glimpse of San Francisco.

Around her the ship creaked and groaned, and the deck swayed slightly. A fine spray curling back from the prow made the rail beneath her gloved hands slick with moisture. The damp smell of seaweed, the taste of salt in the air, the call of the gulls winging about the ship added to the strange stirring inside that at the same time excited and repelled her.

"I'm not going to bury myself in the wilderness," Marianna repeated. "And I won't let Harold bury himself either!" She glanced down at her left hand where the outline of the giant pearl in her betrothal ring was visible beneath the soft leather glove. She remembered vividly the June ball when her stepcousin Harold Von Wooten had placed that ring on her finger. She had been nineteen and an acknowledged belle; he had been twenty-four, with a Harvard degree in his pocket and a solid future in the investment firm of Burgee and Smythe ahead of him. Their families had been thrilled by the news, for the marriage would serve to hold the circle together, and Marianna had been happy to commit her future to a man she had known and trusted all her life.

Then had come the trip to California—a matter of a few months, Harold had said—to invest in a freight line to supply the gold fields, but she remembered the animation in his manner and the gleam in his eye. Indeed, she had thought of him often as the months grew into years, and her prayers changed from "Dear God, keep him safe" to "Lord, bring him back the way he was."

She tried not to imagine the elegant Harold dressed in buckskins or a gold miner's corduroy overalls and living in a tent city or driving a team of freight mules, as her sister's husband did. "Men here may seem rougher than your Philadelphia dandies, but they are more real," she remembered a line from one of her sister's letters and repressed a little shudder. Such sentiments were fine for Gloriana. She had never enjoyed the Philadelphia social world and had laughed at the young men who came courting the Windemere sisters. But Marianna had loved it. A home on a tree-lined boulevard with a comfortable husband who could assure her a continued place in that world was all she had ever wanted. She had made the long journey from the East Coast to make sure that dream would come true. "Harold will be glad to come back home with me," she reassured herself, ignoring the nagging question at the back of her mind: *What if he won't?*

Caught up in her own thoughts, Marianna had missed the first sight of the San Francisco skyline. Now the excited murmurs from her fellow passengers as they pushed forward to the ship's railing called her back to the present. What she saw amazed her.

Where she had expected rude log buildings and canvas tents stood a metropolis. A forest of ship masts crowded a harbor as busy as that of any Eastern sea port. Long wharves reached out into the water. Warehouses lined the docks. And climbing from the water's edge into a ring of surrounding hills were broad avenues and tier upon tier of tall buildings.

"They call it the wickedest city in the world," a deep voice spoke close beside Marianna's ear, and she looked up into the disturbing brown eyes of Cole Taylor. He had introduced himself as an "Old San Franciscan"—one who had lived in the city more than a year—when he boarded the ship at Panama.

"You sound proud of the fact," she answered him almost snappishly. Then, remembering her manners, she added hastily, "That is, doesn't it bother you for people to call your home wicked?"

A lazy grin started at the side of his mouth and spread slowly across the man's deeply tanned face. "Perhaps I'm a bit wicked myself." Cole Taylor looked more than a bit wicked; with his broad black hat set at a rakish angle on his forehead and his black frock coat open over a frilled shirt, string tie, and embroidered vest—to Marianna's unpracticed eye he looked like a river boat gambler. A small scar over his right eye and the slight bump where his nose had been broken kept his face from classic handsomeness, while giving evidence of a life of violence. The frosting of silver at his temples and tiny lines at the corners of his eyes placed his age somewhere over thirty; while broad shoulders and a tall, muscular build hinted at a rugged vitality that seemed to her less than genteel.

"Come, admit it," Cole Taylor smiled more broadly as he read the open contempt as well as reluctant admiration in Marianna's face. "The worse we westerners are, the better you lovely eastern ladies like it. We present a challenge to your reforming instincts."

In spite of her determination not to be provoked, Marianna could not repress a little gasp. Her acquaintance with this man had been forced by the close quarters of the ship and by the need to be civil to one's traveling companions. His great interest in her and her concerns had been obvious to everyone on board, and equally obvious had been his ability to draw her into battles much too heated and personal for propriety. She had determined today to maintain an icy demeanor to show him clearly that their enforced shipboard acquaintance was at an end; however, she could not resist one parting shot: "I have no interest in reforming either your city or you!"

The crew let down the mainsails. The great ship shuddered and its deck lurched, throwing Marianna against Cole Taylor. For an instant she was aware only of the woodsy scent of his shaving soap and the hidden strength in the arm that steadied her. Then he bent close to her ear so that his breath tickled her cheek. "I'm glad you like me the way I am," he said too softly for the passengers pressing around them to hear, "but I don't think I will mind being reformed by you."

Too outraged to speak, Marianna could only glare at him, but before she could pull away, a shrill voice turned all heads in their direction.

"Young man, unhand my niece! Marianna, step away from that man." Pushing her way through the crowd with the help of a plump elbow and a sharp-pointed umbrella was Marianna's formidable Aunt Myriah Von Wooten, Harold's stepmother and the sister of Marianna's father. Built along generous lines, she was an imposing figure in voluminous black skirts and an enormous bonnet that towered fully a foot above her pepper-and-salt hair. Her normally ruddy complexion was mottled with exertion and anger.

"Marianna, your fiancé will be waiting for us." She called the attention of her red-faced niece to the crowd already gathering on the dock, then rounded on the tall Californian with no attempt to lower her voice. "You, sir, would do well to remember that Miss Windemere is engaged to be married to a very influential citizen of this city. I assure you that he will be most offended when I tell him about your forcing your attentions upon her."

The smile on Cole Taylor's lips did not quite reach his eyes, but his voice remained low and steady, almost drawling, as he replied, "If Miss Windemere's fiancé lives in San Francisco, I'm sure he will have heard of an old California custom—claim jumping." Then he tipped his hat and with a great show of courtesy made room for the bristling woman beside her niece.

Meanwhile the *Yankee Clipper* was moving slowly into the harbor. Above the deck, sailors scrambled through the ship's rigging while the mates blew their whistles and shouted orders made unintelligible by the general clamor. Without the wind in its mainsails, the ship's pace was sedate, but rocky, riding on the harbor swells rather than plowing through them. Below, Marianna saw a small boat come alongside and a wiry figure scramble up the rope ladder dangling precariously against the ship's side. "Harbor pilot aboard," a sailor called out, and a deep voice answered from the wheelhouse, inviting the pilot forward.

"With any luck we can collect Harold and be back aboard for the return voyage," Aunt Myriah was saying in a grim voice that noted clearly she was dismissing the Californian from her mind and from discussion. "I have already asked the captain to reserve our cabins." Her faded blue eyes registered a determination that bolstered her niece's flagging confidence.

Still, Marianna could not help asking her aunt the question she had not dared ask herself, "But, Aunt, what if Harold does not want to go home? He never replied to your letter asking him to return, and it's been months since we've heard from him."

Myriah Von Wooten gave her niece a speculative glance that took in the fresh complexion, the tip-tilted nose, and the huge eyes, still misted slightly with tears of humiliation from the scene to which her aunt had subjected her. "That stepson of mine would have to be twice a fool not to come home after you've chased halfway around the world to find him."

Marianna flushed at the implication of her aunt's words. Did everyone view her coming to San Francisco as chasing after Harold? Well, she supposed she was, but surely three years of waiting faithfully for her absent fiancé gave her that right—three years of watching her friends marry, set up housekeeping, and begin their families; three years of being a wallflower and enduring the sympathy of those who knew of Harold's San Francisco adventure and the curiosity of those who did not. Marianna wondered if her fiancé had been as faithful to her as she had been to him.

Her eyes fixed on the green bay waters, lapping against

the side of the ship, Marianna was only dimly aware of the crowd on the dock, shouting greetings, or the halloos of the passengers in reply. But she felt the shock as the *Yankee Clipper* let down its anchor, and she wrinkled her dainty nose in distaste as the fresh sea aromas were exchanged for the fouler smells of the wharves. Whether it were wicked or not, she did not think she was going to like San Francisco.

Make Harold listen to us, God, she found herself praying for the thousandth time. *Don't let him stay here. Make him come back home.* And her mind catalogued a hundred vaguely defined but nonetheless glowingly good works she would be willing to do if only her prayers were answered.

She saw no sign of Harold until the gangplank had been extended and the first passengers, loaded down with baggage, had found their way ashore. And even then, his stepmother saw him first. Pushing his way through the crowd with one hand, he waved his hat with the other. The bright California sun made his smooth blond hair look almost white, and the distance did not prevent Marianna's noticing he had grown a mustache and sideburns and had exchanged his businesslike homburg for a sleek top hat.

He embraced his stepmother first, then dropped a kiss on Marianna's cheek. "I almost forgot how pretty you are," Harold told her. The admiration in his eyes was unmistakable, and his hand lingered on hers for a moment before he followed her aunt to the cabins and their luggage.

"Is that the best he can do after being away from you for three years?"

The mockery in Cole Taylor's tone as much as his words made Marianna blush with embarrassment. He was leaning against the wheelhouse in a lazy posture that suggested he had been watching her for a while.

"Harold is a gentleman. He would not want to embarrass me with a scene," Marianna defended her fiancé, but the defense sounded less than convincing, even to her own ears.

Cole did not reply, yet when he laughed, his eyes lingered on her red lips, suggesting better than words the kind of greeting he considered appropriate between sweethearts.

"Will you tell me where you will be staying and give me permission to call on you?" he asked, still smiling but speaking softly, almost slyly as though he were daring her to see him again. Probably he did not expect Marianna to answer. Certainly she should not have. Perhaps the challenge touched her pride, or maybe she felt a twinge of resentment, not even admitted to herself, at her fiancé's restraint. In any case, before she realized what was happening, Marianna had given the man not only the name of her hotel but also her hand, and he had raised it to his lips.

"Marianna!" Aunt Myriah's shrill voice caused Marianna to jump guiltily, and Harold's frown of disapproval prompted her to pull her hand out of Cole Taylor's lingering grasp. The men greeted each other with distant nods—enough to indicate they knew, but did not particularly like, each other.

"I'm not happy to see you encouraging a man like that," Harold told her sternly when Cole had left the ship.

"I don't know what you mean." Marianna's defense of herself surprised her as much as her fiancé. "He seems a perfect gentleman to me."

Harold's words were cold, but his pale, gray-blue eyes looked hotly angry as he responded. "The man is a perfect scoundrel—the kind of cutthroat charlatan who gives San Francisco a bad name. If it were not for him and the band of pirates that work for him, I could have come home months ago."

An uncomfortably quiet party climbed into Harold's waiting carriage. The luxurious vehicle had thick blue velvet cushions and gleaming brass appointments, including two highly polished lanterns positioned on each side of the coachman's seat. The coachman himself was dressed in black livery that matched the team of sleek, high-spirited horses.

"My employer, Jacques Tremaine, insisted I borrow his carriage," Harold explained to his stepmother, then went on to extol the virtues of a man who was apparently a self-made millionaire and an entrepreneur of staggering proportions with interests in banking, gold mines, shipping, and real estate.

"Are you then no longer with Burgee and Smythe?" Marianna ventured a question. She had often passed the conservative gray stone building in downtown Philadelphia where the firm had its offices and imagined "Von Wooten" added in gold script to the names on the window.

Harold frowned at her as though the question were somehow idiotic. "The opportunities for a man of my background and talents are much greater with Mr. Tremaine," he said—somewhat ostentatiously, Marianna thought. She exchanged a look with her aunt. On this point at least they were in agreement. Harold did not say what position exactly he held with the wealthy Mr. Tremaine, but Marianna gathered from Harold's enthusiastic descriptions that whatever he did entitled him to a large office and an even larger salary. She listened with only half her mind to the conversation between her aunt and fiancé and directed her gaze out the carriage window.

They were on a broad avenue lined with tall buildings and crowded with vehicles. Market Street, Harold called it, pointing proudly to an impressive building fronted by stone pillars, which he said housed Bonanza Enterprises, Mr. Tremaine's corporation. Nearby were the Pacific Stock Exchange, several banks, and the offices of a host of smaller firms, most memorable because their names somehow alluded to gold or mining: Gold Strike Corp., Sierra Gold Mining, Gold Nugget Finance. Everywhere were reminders of the gold rush that had caused San Francisco to boom just six short years earlier, yet there was none of the gold camp atmosphere Marianna had expected. Eastern news stories had described acres of tents and a population of miners, half-crazed with gold fever. What she saw reminded her of Wall Street in New

York. Even the pedestrians were elegant, sporting fashionable, silver-topped canes and wearing high-crowned beaver hats.

"It's unbelievable how much the city has changed in the three short years I have been here," Harold was saying in the same excited tone Marianna remembered from the first time he had told her about San Francisco.

Three "short" years? They had seemed long to her—an eternity of waiting to get on with her life.

"When I arrived, the harbor was filled with rotting ships, abandoned when the crews jumped ship to join the gold rush in 1849. The streets were knee-deep in mud most of the year, and the buildings were made of canvas with false fronts of wood and plaster. The city has burned six times in six years, but each time it has been built back better than ever."

Aunt Myriah gasped, and Marianna shuddered, imagining the buildings around her engulfed in flames.

"The fires have been especially devastating because the streets are paved, as you may have noticed, with wooden planks."

They had not noticed, but both ladies looked nervously from their carriage windows to see the unusual paving stretched between raised walkways, which were also made of wood. They realized then why the noisy clattering of the carriage wheels had changed little since they left the wooden wharf.

"In the last fire whole streets were rivers of flames running out and over the bay as the wharves caught fire," Harold went on with a complete disregard for the effect his words were having on his listeners. He seemed not only proud of what had been accomplished but also exhilarated by the danger and hardships overcome.

He loves this city, Marianna thought and her heart sank. *How can I ask him to leave?* Yet San Francisco did not seem to agree with Harold Von Wooten. Studying him out of the corner of her eye while she looked this way and that at various landmarks he pointed out to them, Marianna noticed his complexion was washed out and his eyes slightly puffy. The lines about his mouth could not be entirely hidden by the silvery mustache, and his chest beneath the elegant broadcloth coat seemed sunken, as though he had recently lost a great deal of weight. Unconsciously she found herself comparing her fiancé with Cole Taylor. *Harold is more handsome, but Cole Taylor is more manly.* She startled herself with the observation, then smiled ruefully as she recalled her sister Gloriana's comments about the "real" men of the West. *Watch out,* Marianna scolded herself. *You don't want to fall victim to this western fever.*

Just then a heavily loaded streetcar rumbled past their carriage. Bright red with yellow trim, the car was open all around and drawn by two large Clydesdales. Leaning forward to watch the car's progress, Marianna found herself looking straight into the twinkling eyes of Cole Taylor. He was clinging with one hand to a strap that hung from the roof of the car; his other hand grasped a large leather bag. Unable to wave or salute, he winked at her—a slow meaningful wink that turned Marianna's face red and reminded her the man had almost admitted to being wicked—and Marianna thought she saw him mouth the words, "See you soon."

I should never have come here, she realized suddenly with the clear insight that sometimes comes only when it is too late.

CHAPTER 2

CALIFORNIA GOLD! The words were magic in the East where newspapers had fanned the flames of gold fever with accounts of twenty-pound nuggets, streams running yellow with gold, and fabulous mother lodes that overnight turned a former bricklayer or farmer or New York street washer into a multimillionaire. And San Francisco had been at the heart of the legendary gold rush. Here the miners had outfitted themselves for the trek into gold country, and here they had returned to spend their riches. "Miners believe it's bad luck to leave Frisco with gold dust in their pokes," one reporter had written. The size and magnificence of the city that had sprung to life in just six short years attested to the lavishness of the miners' spending.

"The gold rush is over, but the building goes on. Fortunes are still to be made in San Francisco," Harold told his aunt and fiancée over a sumptuous dinner in a hotel that rivaled Philadelphia's finest. Aunt Myriah murmured something polite but she gave her niece a sharp look that said clearly, "We have to talk."

For three hours they had exclaimed over the history, marveled at the prosperity, and admired the views of the fabulous Bay City, and for three hours Marianna had felt her spirits sinking. Her feet and legs ached from climbing the steep streets that plunged straight up and down the city's many hills. Her skin felt raw and chapped from the stiff Pacific winds. And deep inside she felt overcome and even humiliated by what she had seen.

Where Marianna had expected to find tents and dirt trails, she had seen brick buildings and paved thoroughfares. Where she had expected rough miners, she had found polished gentlemen—many of them exuding a cosmopolitan elegance to match their French, British, or German accents. Moreover, if the truth were known, Marianna had expected to be an undisputed belle in the West—the epitome of eastern fashion and sophistication; instead, she felt very young and naïve and almost dowdy.

She had caught Harold's quick appraisal and dismissal of her dinner costume when he had met them at the foot of the hotel's grand staircase. Now glancing at the elaborate gowns and the glittering jewels of the diners around them, she could understand his reaction. Her simple rose-colored silk with its tiny puffed sleeves and modest neckline looked almost schoolgirlish beside the low-cut Paris creations. The creamy cameo—her one piece of real jewelry—had seemed elegant tied around her neck on a velvet ribbon, but now she found herself fingering it self-consciously and wishing for a ruby pendant or at least a strand of pearls. She wondered what it would feel like to have plumes in her hair, to let one curl flirtatiously around her ear, just touching her cheek, or to tuck several into a crown of curls where they would dip and wave softly with every movement of her head.

Tomorrow I could go to a San Francisco shop and get a new outfit—not anything too extravagant but just enough so that I won't feel out of place. Her aunt was paying for the trip, but her father had given her some spending money—for "fripperies," he had said—though she doubted he had had Paris dresses in mind. For a moment she tried to imagine herself in an off-the-shoulder white satin gown with a necklet and tiara of pearls like those worn by the beautiful, if somewhat loud, blonde at the next table. She had noticed Harold's eyes stray in the woman's direction again and again during dinner, and his approval and appreciation had been unmistakable. Would his eyes spark with so much excitement if she touched her lips with rouge, wore a plunging neckline, and threw her head back when she laughed?

Marianna sighed and pushed the tiny onions and peas, barely touched, around on her plate. She was only fooling herself. No amount of window dressing would make her fit into this exotic place. She was a strait-laced minister's daughter from Philadelphia and as out of place as a sweet pea in a bouquet of hothouse orchids.

Her eyes found the untouched glass of champagne beside her plate and then her aunt's half-filled and Harold's frequently emptied glass. Aunt Myriah never touched liquor, but she had confided in Marianna that since they were far from home and friends, no one would know if they pretended to go along with her stepson's lifestyle, but only, of course, until they could bring him to his senses. Several times during the evening, her aunt had glanced pointedly at Marianna's glass, but she had carefully ignored the hint, pledging toasts with little sips of water.

"Father must never find out about this," Marianna thought as she noticed the flush in her aunt's cheeks and detected a slight tremor in her shrill voice. The Reverend Windemere had always admired his elder sister for her ramrod backbone and uncompromising principles. "Myriah never bends," he was fond of saying. Probably, though, he would understand better than anyone how a parent's concern for a straying child might push her to behave desperately, without concern for other people or for her own self-respect.

But was the situation that desperate? Was Harold straying recklessly or was he simply stretching his wings and making the most of his freedom for the short while before he settled down to a life of responsibility and respectability? At one time Marianna could have answered that question unhesitatingly, but now she was not sure. In the dazzling light of the hotel's chandeliers,

Harold looked worldly and totally unfamiliar. His evening clothes were dashing and well-cut, giving him the air of a gentleman of leisure rather than a hard-working businessman. When he spoke to the waiter, his tone was almost haughty. The French phrases on the menu had rolled off his tongue with the ease of constant use.

Why, I hardly know him anymore! Marianna startled herself with the thought, and she looked quickly at her aunt, wondering whether the older woman shared her growing bewilderment. If she did, Aunt Myriah gave no sign but began determinedly to bring her stepson up to date on the lives of every relative, friend, or nodding acquaintance they had left behind in Philadelphia.

"I need not tell you, of course, what our dear little Marianna has been doing. Many's the time I have seen this child sitting quietly at a party, content to wait patiently on the sidelines until a certain someone comes home again." Aunt Myriah cast a coy look at her blushing niece and patted her hand sympathetically. "You needn't pretend, my dear. I know how hard it has been watching all of your friends marry and have babies. But I'm sure you will not have much longer to wait. Harold will do the right thing by you. He's his father's son after all, and a Von Wooten never goes back on his word."

Her face as rosy as her dress, Marianna ventured a quick glance at her fiancé. She fully expected to find him as embarrassed as she, but instead a rather self-satisfied smirk touched his lips.

"Perhaps the two of you would like to be alone to discuss your plans," Aunt Myriah prodded relentlessly. Then ignoring Marianna's panicky protest, the older woman jerked awkwardly to her feet and bustled noisily from the restaurant, her ample black skirts over a round hoop sweeping a wide path and her arm beckoning imperiously for a waiter to attend her.

She left behind an awkward silence that stretched uncomfortably. Marianna searched her mind frantically for something to say that would relieve the embarrassment—something light and offhand that would erase the picture of the blushing cast-off maiden her aunt had so effectively created. But she was too furious to think.

Harold's attention seemed to be fixed on his dessert. Spooning a large portion of apricot mousse into his mouth, he did not meet her eyes, but the same what-a-big-man-am-I smile played about his lips, and Marianna could see he was enjoying being the pursued rather than the pursuer. That she might find the situation humiliating he did not seem to notice or care.

Unable to bear the silence any longer, Marianna ventured a comment about the magnificence of the restaurant, then gave herself a mental kick for the banality of her words. "Have you ever seen so much gold?" She went on, chattering now but determined to allow no further conversational gaps. "Gold leaf on those plaster moldings along the walls, gold thread in the heavy Louis XIV draperies, gold handles on the cutlery. And the carpets! I feel as if I am sinking into them."

Harold offered no reply but glanced obediently around him. *At least he could try to help keep the conversation going,* Marianna thought indignantly and shifted resolutely to discussing the food. She wondered aloud about the ingredients of the apricot mousse, about the source of the fruit and the fresh peas. She imagined a variety of spices used in preparing the bouillabaisse she had hardly tasted and speculated about the cooking time for a custard she had only pushed around on her plate.

"You are suddenly very talkative," Harold said, finally, a glint of amusement in his eye. "All day you barely say a word and suddenly you're Little Miss Chatterbox. Does being under Myriah's thumb oppress you so much that when you are away from her, you break loose?"

Speechless for a moment, Marianna did not miss the sneer in Harold's voice or the way he had carefully avoided adding his usual "Mother" before his stepmother's first name.

"I am not blaming you, you know. She affects me the same way . . . always has. Why, the old harridan has only to walk in the room and I find myself sitting up straighter and checking my tie to be sure it's not crooked." As if to emphasize his new freedom, Harold leaned back in his chair and loosened his collar; his harsh grating laugh reminded Marianna he had been drinking.

"You're being unkind," Marianna said finally. "You know you're her whole world since your father died. She would do anything for you."

Harold had the grace to color slightly, and he pushed away his glass as though he had just realized its effect on him. "I know," he said quietly. "But I get so tired of her endlessly interfering in my life."

Marianna caught her breath, but she managed to keep her voice steady. "Like her coming here and bringing me?"

Harold's eyes met hers steadily, and his hand reached across the table to cover her trembling one, but the words were honest, chilling her heart. "Like her coming here and bringing you."

For a second the room with its glittering crowd and glittering atmosphere went into a spin. Then she heard Harold suggest they take the air on the veranda. With a poise and detachment that surprised even herself, Marianna accepted the waiter's help in rising from the table. She stood quietly as Harold draped her gauze stole around her shoulders and even managed a smile as he led her in a roundabout path to accommodate her hooped skirts toward the arched doors that opened on the hotel's gardens.

But all the while something inside was crying, *He doesn't want me here. He wishes I hadn't come.*

Outside the night was glorious. A giant moon like a polished medallion of California gold rode majestically over a harbor filled with the winking lights and ghostly masts of ships. Stars bright and clear, undimmed by the smoke of the great eastern cities, filled the dark dome of the sky.

Near at hand gas lights flickered in street lamps. The mingled scents of honeysuckle and roses filled the air. A tiered marble fountain, gleaming in the soft light, splashed musically, its cascading water muffling the sounds from the dining room and the steady nighttime murmurs of the city.

Leading her to a marble bench beside the fountain, Harold turned away briefly to light a cigarello. Marianna watched curiously as he cupped his hands around his match and nursed a glow of tiny embers at the end of his cigar. A heavy gray smoke drifted into the shadows, and a sharp, pungent smell blotted out the scent of flowers. Harold inhaled deeply, coughed, then inhaled again before he turned back to her.

Marianna fanned the smoke away unobtrusively from her face and tried not to think too much about his not having asked her permission to smoke. Probably he was too agitated by what he wanted to say to her to remember the common courtesies. Oddly enough she felt calm, almost unnaturally so. Clasping her hands together in her lap, she looked up, her head tilted courageously as though she intended to take whatever came on the chin, and silently willed Harold to be the first to speak. He, however, seemed contented just to smoke his cigar and look at her.

She might not be ultrafashionable or sophisticated, but Harold's eyes said clearly, she was a picture in the moonlight. The admiration bolstered Marianna's flagging self-confidence, though she reminded herself sternly, *Now he doesn't have the blonde to look at.*

"I don't know how to say this to you," he began at last, and Marianna braced herself. Sitting down beside her, he took her left hand in his. Briefly he studied the effect of his pearl ring on her hand and frowned. But all he said was, "I wanted to give you a diamond; Myriah said you preferred the pearl."

Marianna started to open her mouth in a denial but quickly changed her mind. What did it matter that she would have rather had the diamond? It was still not her favorite. She had always dreamed of a sapphire engagement ring chosen lovingly to match her eyes.

"You understand how it is between Myriah and me. Oh, I know you're right that she genuinely cares for me and has my best interests at heart. And I won't deny that sometimes she is right." The meaningful squeeze of her hand sent pinpricks of alarm through Marianna as she wondered suddenly whose idea her engagement to Harold had been.

"But we don't talk." Harold bit down on his cigar in frustration, then unthinkingly he sent choking clouds of smoke in her direction. "She won't listen to me. She didn't listen when I wrote and told her not to come here, so I'm going to say this to you instead and hope and pray you can persuade her; you've got to get out of San Francisco. It's not safe."

The menace behind Harold's words sent shivers up and down her spine, and Marianna found herself glancing nervously over her shoulder as he escorted her to her hotel room.

"The *Yankee Clipper* sails in one week," he told her at the door of the suite she shared with her aunt. "I want you to be on it." Then he kissed her passionately and thoroughly, leaving Marianna disheveled but strangely unmoved. *I suppose Cole Taylor would approve of that kiss.* The thought popped unbidden into her mind, and Marianna blushed hotly.

In the sitting room, as Marianna had expected, Aunt Myriah waited impatiently. A tea tray with nearly empty plates of macaroons and filled date cookies was on the table. Her aunt had taken off her shoes, and her stocking-clad feet, large and rather knobby with bunions caused by a lifetime of wearing pinching shoes, rested comfortably on a needlepoint ottoman. Her smug smile exuded self-satisfaction as she asked eagerly, "What did he say? When's the wedding? Shall I confirm the passage for all three of us aboard the *Yankee Clipper?*"

Marianna felt suddenly very weary. "No wedding," she said in a flat voice, "not now and maybe never. I don't know. He wants us to leave as soon as possible. He says we're in danger here."

"But is he coming with us?"

"No . . . at least I don't think so. He didn't say he would."

Aunt Myriah said nothing while she digested the

information. Then with the air of an old campaigner, she stood, squared her shoulders, and poured herself another cup of tea. "We have a week," she began with a shrewd glance at her niece. "That should be plenty of time. Tomorrow morning we'll see about some new clothes for you and maybe a new hairstyle. I'll get tickets for the opera and call on a few acquaintances so we will be invited out. Then we'll set about sweeping that stepson of mine off his feet."

Marianna shook her head, too tired to argue. How could she explain after traveling so many thousands of miles that she did not want to chase after Harold, that she felt she hardly knew him anymore, and what she knew she was not sure she liked?

"We'll plan it all in the morning," her aunt reassured Marianna in a determinedly cheerful tone. "Now off to bed. You mustn't neglect your beauty rest if you want to dazzle a young man."

He seemed dazzled enough but not by me, Marianna wanted to say but did not. Instead she started obediently to her room, then turned and asked quietly, though she dreaded hearing the answer, "Aunt, did Harold answer your letter asking him to return home? Did he ask us not to come?"

Myriah Von Wooten looked uncomfortable; but she answered forthrightly enough. "He did answer something about unsettled times and the streets being unsafe for a woman alone. But he had no idea I would be bringing you. I was sure his delight at seeing his fiancée again would override any objections."

Marianna hesitated, then almost whispered her question, "Did you choose my engagement ring?"

Her aunt looked startled, then colored and dropped her eyes. "I have always intended you to have my pearls when you married. The ring is a perfect match."

Marianna had assumed hers was the perfect romance. She had known Harold all her life. They had the same friends, even the same family. And best of all they had seemed meant for each other. She had often thought about how Harold must have loved her for years, waiting only for her to grow up before he declared himself.

"You have been a romantic idiot," Marianna scolded the reflection in her dressing table mirror sternly to keep the tears glistening in her eyes from falling. Aunt Myriah had obviously suggested that her stepson court her niece, and since Harold's father, Harold Von Wooten II, had left the purse strings securely in his wife's hands, the young man had probably had no alternative. Of course, he said that Marianna was the one thing his stepmother had been right about, and he had kissed her tonight as though he meant it.

"But nothing's the way I thought it was," she told the looking-glass girl and let a tear or two of self-pity roll down her cheek. She felt half inclined to blame God. Hadn't she prayed for Harold to come home unchanged? Hadn't she promised any number of good works in exchange? What more did God want?

"Nothing is wrong with wanting the same kind of life all my friends have," she assured herself. But the question slipped into her consciousness from somewhere deep inside, *Is that the life the Lord wants for me?*

Caught up in her own inner turmoil, Marianna had taken the pins from her hair and brushed her curls into a glossy mantle that fell about her shoulders before she noticed the little note propped against the mirror. Her name was written in a bold, unfamiliar hand across an envelope of hotel stationery. Probably the bell captain had brought it up while they were at dinner and left it where she would be sure to notice.

But who would be writing to her? She didn't know anyone in San Francisco, or did she?

Her fingers trembled slightly as she tore the envelope open.

Must see you right away. Will call tomorrow at 11:00 to take you for a buggy ride. Wear something warm.

Cole

The message held nothing particularly loving, but it boosted Marianna's spirits considerably. At least one man did not want her to go back to Philadelphia.

Ordinarily she would have resented the presumptuous

tone of the note. In fact, a few short hours before she might have ripped it into tiny pieces and sent it back to him or perhaps arranged to be leaving the hotel exactly at 11:00 when he would be sure to see her. But the humiliations of the past few hours had made the aggressive Californian's attentions seem enticingly welcome in retrospect. And finding a sheet of hotel stationery, Marianna quickly penned a reply.

Dear Mr. Taylor,

Your mysterious message has aroused my curiosity. I will meet you in the square before the hotel at 9:30.

Marianna Windemere

P.S. If it seems cool to me, I will, of course, wear suitable clothes.

Sealing the envelope with wax to guard against prying eyes, she tiptoed to her door, then across the sitting room to leave the note in the message tray outside the door. A bellboy would find it in the morning, along with the gratuity she had left underneath. She had no idea where it should be delivered and so had left the address blank, but somehow she felt certain that everyone in San Francisco must know Cole Taylor.

Harold will be furious, she told herself with something suspiciously like a giggle. And a little smile was on her lips as she crawled wearily between the extravagant silk sheets on her four-poster bed. *Papa would be shocked at so much luxury,* she thought, remembering the rough muslin sheets on her bed at home, but as she drifted off to sleep, she would have gladly exchanged the silk and her lavish surroundings for her own bed in her own room back home.

CHAPTER 3

MARIANNA WOKE WITH A START. A soft morning glow filtered through heavy draperies, covering the quilted bedspread with pale spiderwebs of light. With her head half buried in a silk-covered down pillow, Marianna could not see anyone, but she sensed a presence in the room. The spicy aroma of jasmine drifted to her from a flowered china teapot on a tray beside her bed. A faint rustling sound like someone tiptoeing across the carpet reached her ears.

"Who's there?" she asked, sitting up quickly.

The question startled a tiny Oriental maid who had been trying to light a fire in the fireplace. She dropped the match and tried to retrieve it. The little cry of pain that escaped the girl's tightly pressed lips brought Marianna out of her bed and across the room. It took her only a few minutes to cool the burned fingers with water and to apply a soothing salve from a first-aid kit, which her mother had insisted she pack in the top tray of her trunk. By then Marianna had learned that the girl's name was Mi Ling, that she lived in Chinatown with her father and three young brothers, and that she was very much afraid of losing her job.

"I am not good maid," Mi Ling confessed humbly, her

eyes downcast and her musically singsong voice trembling.

"I'm sure you are a perfectly marvelous maid," Marianna reassured her, gently pushed the distraught girl into a chair, and pressed a cup of the fragrant tea into her hands.

Mi Ling gave her a shy, frightened smile. But tears glistened in the huge almond-shaped eyes, and her quick glances toward the door spoke clearly of her fear of being discovered drinking tea when she should be working. Sensing something more than burned fingers behind the girl's nervousness, Marianna avoided probing, but she could not help noticing the thinness of the shoulders, arms, and legs beneath the maid's shapeless gray costume. The outfit lacked only the pointed round coolie hat to match the pictures Marianna had seen in drawings of Chinese peasants. And Mi Ling was trying unsuccessfully to hide a bruised wrist beneath a too-short sleeve.

"This morning is disaster," Mi Ling explained shakily as she brushed away a tear. "My clumsiness and forgetting cause many problems. Wash bowl in room of very rich man overturn, bringing much-deserved punishment. Tear in esteemed opera singer's favorite dress not mended. I forget to deliver paper to bellboy captain. Now I wake you."

Whether Mi Ling's duties legitimately included all the things she mentioned, Marianna doubted, but she had no doubt the shy maid had been soundly punished for each real or supposed infraction.

"Sometime Mi Ling very stupid," the girl told her with a little smile and a self-denigrating shrug that made Marianna bristle to her defense.

"I think you should find another job where they treat you better."

"Oh, no! I not want other job. I become good maid, then no more punishment." The sheer terror in the Oriental girl's eyes startled Marianna into silence, but she wondered whether any amount of good service would prevent her abuse.

"I go now. Thank you for tea."

Marianna watched curiously as the girl scurried toward the door with tiny, graceful steps. At the dresser she stopped briefly and touched the delicate undergarments Marianna had flung there carelessly the night before.

"May I wash for you?"

Marianna nodded, although she had intended to wash them herself. *I can pay her extra for the work,* she thought, happy to find a better use than Paris fashions for the money her father had given her.

Growing up in Philadelphia, Marianna had rarely encountered people of other races. Her own family usually hired German or Irish immigrants to help with the house or yard work, and the people they met socially all seemed to come from the same background. She had, of course, seen black people on the city streets, and once a missionary had brought an elderly Cherokee to her father's church to make his mission's work seem more real. But she had never before had the chance to talk face to face with someone whose skin color was different from her own.

Not surprisingly, she had found the experience exciting. Mi Ling had an exotic air of mystery that made Marianna want to know more about her—about her homeland, about the Chinatown where she lived now. More importantly, though, Marianna had felt fiercely protective of the Oriental girl. Having been raised in a minister's family, she had a well-developed sense of justice. Perhaps she was not suited to the life of a missionary like her sister Gloriana, but she cared deeply about human suffering.

Wishing she could do something, Marianna poured herself a cup of the now tepid jasmine tea and climbed back onto the bed. Decorated in creamy whites and the ever-present California gold, the room around her looked rich and elegant. Soft filtered light made the trim on the furnishings glow. The matching ruffles around the skirt and canopy of the four-poster bed looked like white clouds.

Marianna shivered. A tremor of guilt? She could not escape the uncomfortable feeling that the hotel's luxury might contrast starkly with the poverty in other parts of San Francisco.

Still, it was surprisingly chilly for a summer morning—the effect perhaps of the Pacific winds that swept so relentlessly over the city. The fire Mi Ling had not remembered to light would have felt good, but, Marianna told herself, the thick down quilt on her bed warmed her feet just as well.

She supposed she could speak to the hotel manager about his patrons' abuse of the maid. She was certain one of the irate guests Mi Ling had mentioned was responsible for the bruise on the girl's wrist. Yet what if the manager condoned such treatment? Would Mi Ling lose her job due to Marianna's interference? The very idea of finding a new position had terrified the girl, although Marianna imagined that a growing city with so few women and so many luxurious hotels must have a demand for maids.

Perhaps Cole Taylor could help the girl.

The name brought back the incidents of the past evening with a rush, and Marianna remembered with horror her impulsive note to the San Franciscan.

Had she really promised to meet him? Her aunt would be furious.

Hoping against hope, she raced on bare feet out of her bedroom and across the sitting room. But the message tray was empty. The note was gone. Probably even now it was being delivered.

"Well, there's nothing to do now but keep the appointment," she said more bravely than she felt.

The ornate, Louis XIV clock on the mantel—Marianna wondered whether the trimming were real gold leaf or the less expensive copper imitation called ormolu—set the time at 8:30. She would have to hurry. Fortunately Aunt Myriah was a late and heavy sleeper. Perhaps she would be able to meet Cole Taylor, make some kind of excuse, and return before she was missed.

It was 9:45 before Marianna slipped nervously through a side door of the hotel. Everything that could go wrong had gone wrong. Instead of falling easily into its usual smooth-topped style, her hair had rioted around her face, peeking in a dark fringe of curls from under the rim of her bonnet. The conservative brown walking dress, with which she had hoped to set a somber tone for the encounter, had been too wrinkled to wear, and she had been forced to don a cheery yellow summer frock that made her look ready for a ride in the country or a picnic in the park. Two of the buttons on her soft kid boots had defied the button hook to remain unfastened, gaping uncomfortably over her ankles. Her bonnet strings had come off and had to be pinned in place.

"And now I'm late," Marianna grumbled to herself as she waited for a break in traffic so that she could cross to the square. She had left a note for her aunt, saying she had gone out on business and would return as soon as she could. Since she had no business and no friends in San Francisco, she could only imagine her aunt's horrified reaction if she were not back before the note were read.

She had been standing for several minutes before Marianna realized that the traffic on the avenue showed no sign of slowing down to let her cross. Glancing around her in bewilderment, she spotted Cole Taylor motioning to her from the other side.

"Come here," she thought he said above the din of rolling wheels and trotting horses. It did not look safe, but with no other way to cross, she supposed she would have to try it. Probably San Franciscans with their love of adventure thought nothing of doing this very thing ten times a day. And gathering her skirts and her courage, Marianna dodged into the traffic.

She was halfway across and trying to catch her breath as a huge dray thundered past when she felt a strong arm encircle her waist and she was propelled to the other side.

"Why didn't you wait for me like I told you?" Cole Taylor was demanding. Fear had darkened his brown eyes to a near black and his face looked pale despite the golden tan. He gave her an angry little shake, but he did not take his arm away from her waist.

"I thought you said to come," Marianna explained breathlessly. "Isn't that the way all San Franciscans cross the street?" She was uncomfortably aware of the arm still around her, but she was too busy explaining her actions to protest.

A reluctant smile spread across Cole's face. He tipped his hat back and, glancing down, let his eyes take in her long sweeping skirts draped bell-like over her moderate-sized walking hoop and the tiny high-heeled boots just visible beneath them. "Well, I suppose we do," he admitted finally. "But since most San Franciscans are men, I guess we never got around to considering that it might be inconvenient for ladies to cross that way. I'll take it up with the Board of Aldermen at our next meeting."

Marianna did not know whether he was joking or not. What would Cole Taylor have to do with the Board of Aldermen? It seemed too completely out of character. So she let his promise pass without comment. Searching her mind for an excuse to cut short their talk and return to the hotel, she hardly noticed she was being led through the wrought-iron fence that bordered Portsmouth Square, past the marble benches and grassy plots at its center, and into a waiting buggy.

"The impressive structure soaring four stories above us is City Hall," Cole told her, pointing to a mammoth building occupying most of one side of the square. He seemed amused at her obvious amazement, and recalling some of their shipboard conversations, Marianna winced at the ignorance that had made her ask how San Franciscans kept warm and dry in their canvas tents and whether they held barn dances for entertainment.

Trying to appear nonchalant, Marianna pointed to an elaborate four-story building next to the courthouse and asked, "What kind of place is that?"

To her surprise Cole frowned and looked uncomfortable. Then he told her briefly, "That's the El Dorado."

"And what is an El Dorado?" she prodded playfully, wondering what there could be about such a magnificent palace to embarrass a man like Cole Taylor.

He glanced at her quickly as though he thought she might be teasing him. Then with a rough edge of exasperation in his voice, he said, "It's what the newspapers refer to euphemistically as a pleasure palace. It features gambling, drinking, and, uh, other vices."

Marianna turned on the buggy seat to get a better view as they rolled past. "Next to City Hall?" she asked in a shocked whisper.

"Next to City Hall and across the square from your own highly respectable hotel."

After that Marianna did not feel equal to asking any more questions. Touring San Francisco for the second time in two days, she found that the face of the city had changed with the face of her guide. Harold had shown her its wealth—Market Street, the stock exchange, Park Place, and the mansions of the rich. Cole Taylor leaned more to its exotic side—to the things that made San Francisco different from any other city Marianna had visited.

He showed her the French opera house where famous European stars had sung. He showed her a store ship—one of the vessels abandoned when its crew joined the gold rush in '49 and later hauled on shore to help with the building shortage. He stopped and let her examine the tough redwood planks that paved the major thoroughfares and told her about the groves of giant trees along the coast to the north.

But he did not show her Chinatown.

"Too dangerous," was all he said after she told him about meeting Mi Ling and about her suddenly conceived desire to visit the girl's mysterious-sounding home. Yet he did promise to try to help.

"You have to understand that I may not be able to do anything," Cole explained earnestly. "The Celestials, as we call them, are hard to get close to. They have their own laws and their own customs and they don't like interfering Americans. Can't say I blame them the way they are treated most of the time. But I'll do my best."

They had driven to the top of Telegraph Hill—the rounded peak from which signal fires and semaphore flags transmitted messages to ships coming into the harbor. Below and to the west of them the city marched bravely down its steep plunging hills to the thickets of ship masts crowded along the wharves. The straight, even streets and the neatly plotted rectangles of buildings, parks, and yards were mute testimony to the foresight that had prevented a boomtown of haphazard growth.

"Look familiar?" Cole asked.

To her own surprise, Marianna nodded yes. "But I can't quite put my finger on it."

"You should. That's your hometown down there. In '48 some dreamer took the original plot of Philadelphia and laid it out right over the hills and tidal flats. Of course he never stopped to worry about how steep the grades on some of his arrow-straight avenues might be."

Marianna laughed. "But what a small price to pay for a city of elegance and beauty."

Cole grinned. "So you like my city after all."

"How can I help it when your founding fathers had the good taste to choose my home as a model?"

They laughed together and then sat quietly, drinking in the beautiful scene. Around the hilltop, wheeling flights of gulls dived and climbed, their shrill cries haunting and strangely appealing. Beyond the city the bay stretched blue and vast like the sky; its white-capped waves gleamed brightly in the sun. And to the north and east, marked by two pillars of towering white clouds, was the entrance to San Francisco Bay, the Golden Gateway to California.

"Oh, it's glorious," Marianna breathed, lifting her face to feel the sea breeze and to let the warmth of the sun sink in.

Cole moved closer to her on the buggy seat. His arm came around her shoulders, and, tipping back his hat, he bent slowly toward her. Fascinated, like someone caught in the slow motion of a dream, Marianna noticed a thick fringe of black lashes—too long and lavish to be wasted on a man—the deep tan of his smoothly shaved cheek, a tiny scar at the corner of his lower lip, pulling it upward in a little half smile. And then her eyes closed in a long breathless kiss.

Cole had pulled away and was studying her with amused intensity before Marianna remembered to open her eyes again. Her breath seemed caught in her throat, and her hands were trembling, but except for a slight huskiness in his voice, he seemed unaffected.

"I won't do that again while you're wearing another man's ring," he said with a little laugh that might have been an ungentlemanly crow of victory at her flattering reaction to his kiss or a humorless chuckle at his own folly.

Finding her voice at last, Marianna lashed out, "I don't know why you're concerned about my engagement now. It has never bothered you before."

"But I had to make sure you had something for comparison." Cole's dark eyes danced with teasing lights. "Now that I've had a fair hearing, I can be more honorable and trust your own good taste to make a choice."

Too furious to talk, Marianna felt her hand swing up in a stinging slap, but Cole caught it before the open palm reached his face. "Stop it, Marianna," he said sternly, giving her a little shake. "Now let's sit quietly for a few minutes until we both get control of ourselves."

He did not release her hand but held it securely in his own strong fingers. Glancing cautiously at him from the corner of her downcast eyes, Marianna detected a tightening in the muscles along his jaw and what might have been a sigh or just a deep breath.

Finally he turned back to her with a look of mingled sorrow and regret. "Marianna, I think I have made it clear how I feel about you. When I first saw you on shipboard, I thought you were the loveliest girl I had ever met, and after all those weeks at sea with you, I was sure of it. That's what makes this the hardest thing I have ever done.

"Marianna, I want you to go home. Go back to Philadelphia on the *Yankee Clipper*. San Francisco is no place for you right now."

CHAPTER 4

MARIANNA WAS TOTALLY BEWILDERED. In less than twenty-four hours two attractive men had kissed her passionately and told her to go home to Philadelphia.

What's wrong with me? she wondered as Cole drove his horse at a rapid trot—obviously eager to be rid of her—back to the hotel on Portsmouth Square. She was not unattractive; in fact, she had been considered a beauty in Philadelphia, though she had personally considered her brunette good looks no more than passable. Raised in a family of pretty girls, she had always longed for her sister Juliana's fair hair and slim figure or for her sister Gloriana's elegant height and perfect complexion.

Still, she had read admiration in Cole Taylor's eyes and in Harold's. What was the problem? Was it her personality? Marianna admitted to a certain single-mindedness, even to a possibly annoying insistence on having her own way. But her way had included returning to Philadelphia—something she would be only too happy to do as long as no one was pushing her into it.

She had chased halfway around the world after Harold, and she had defied her aunt and her fiancé to be with Cole Taylor, not to mention allowing him—and she had to admit she *had* allowed it—the unprecedented privilege of a kiss. After all she had done, the least both men could do was beg her to stay in San Francisco.

Meanwhile, Cole was telling her about a wave of lawlessness and disorder that had swept the city since he had left it six months earlier. In May a gambler had used a tiny derringer he had hidden up his sleeve to shoot a prominent citizen. The gambler had been jailed briefly, tried, and released after his friends bribed the jury. Outraged San Franciscans had reacted with fury and violence; vigilante committees had been formed, and the murderer had been seized and hanged.

"Law and order have broken down completely. During the day the authorities still appear to be in control, but at night gangs of cutthroats and vigilantes rule the city, and no one can tell well-meaning citizens from thieves and murderers." The concern in Cole's voice and his worried looks as he explained the danger might have been reassuring if Marianna had been paying attention. However, her thoughts were elsewhere, and her eyes were fixed vaguely on the city streets thronged with men.

On horseback, in carriages, along the sidewalk—everywhere she saw men. Some wore top hats and tails; some, sombreros and overalls. She saw bearded men and clean-shaven men, men with long fuzzy sideburns and men with hair longer than hers, curled vainly over a beaded and fringed buckskin coat or matted above a knotted red kerchief.

Women, if they appeared at all, did so briefly, drawing every eye in their direction, or they banded together in small groups and walked determinedly, looking neither to the right nor to the left. Marianna was conscious of heads turning and low whistles mixed with some rude guffaws as she rode past, and she realized uncomfortably how unpleasant the streets of San Francisco might be if she were not accompanied by a man like Cole Taylor.

He, of course, was in his element, and Marianna could not resist a twinge of resentment at a world in which she could be so alien, while he was so obviously at home.

They were nearing Portsmouth Square when she heard a sharp cry. A slim figure clad in gray and sporting a long black pigtail was struggling with a mob of men who looked like burly sailors. Something about the long thin arms and legs flailing at the men struck a cord of memory. Then Marianna spotted the bundle of laundry clutched tightly against a shapeless gray tunic.

"That's Mi Ling, the hotel maid." Marianna grabbed Cole's arm and pointed in horror.

Yelling for her to tie the horse, Cole vaulted from the buggy and around an open carriage that had stopped in the middle of the street. The occupant of that carriage was an elegant gentleman dressed all in black with his top hat set at a rakish angle on smooth pomaded locks. He seemed to be watching what was happening with a cool detachment that was incomprehensible to Marianna.

"Why aren't you helping? Oh, please help them," she called to the gentleman. He appeared almost amused by the suggestion, and the piercing eyes that raked over her made Marianna shudder involuntarily. Then, with a little shrug, the elegant stranger stood, smiled and bowed in her direction. After descending from his carriage, he waded into the fray.

With two men against the bullies, the odds were better but by no means even. Cole dispatched one man with hammer blows. Another he pushed into a watering trough where helpful bystanders kept the ruffian off-balance and unable to stand. The stranger did not bother to use his fists but struck at his opponents with devastating sweeps of an ebony walking stick.

The battle lasted no more than a few minutes, but it seemed like hours to Marianna. She had not seen a fist fight since her brothers had tangled with the boys next door, and she had never seen men fight. The difference was awesome. The blows resounded with a force that made her wince. Faces and fists were bloody. Heads cracked as they hit the wooden planking of the street.

Forgetting to tie the horse, Marianna pushed her way through the crowd that had gathered quickly around the combatants. The watchers were boisterous, shouting encouragement, booing, and generally enjoying the show, but none seemed inclined to help.

"Why?" one man responded to Marianna's demand that someone assist the outnumbered fighters. "They're doing just fine."

And they were. Finally, the last bully was vanquished, and the victors shook hands while the crowd cheered.

"Can you beat that?" Marianna overheard the excited talk. "Cole Taylor and Jacques Tremaine shaking hands! I never thought I'd see the day."

Tremaine escorted a trembling Mi Ling to Marianna. "Mademoiselle, it was a pleasure to fight for you," he murmured as he bent gallantly over her hand. His speech held only a trace of French accent, intoning the vowels and lingering over the *s*'s pleasantly. Again, Marianna sensed a trace of amusement and something more in the eyes that held hers appraisingly, and she caught her breath.

Of the two, Cole had definitely gotten the worst of the battle. He had a large cut beneath his left eye, and the skin over the knuckles on his right hand had split open.

"Let's go," he told Marianna gruffly, and she realized she had been staring as the unruffled Tremaine fastidiously brushed some dust from his boots, settled his top hat once more at a jaunty angle, and stepped into his carriage, still the perfect picture of an elegant gentleman.

"Wasn't it fortunate Mr. Tremaine was here to help?" Marianna said enthusiastically.

"Amazing," Cole growled and then added under his breath, "especially since those were his men we were fighting."

Marianna was startled by the charge, but she quickly dismissed it. Obviously hard feelings lay between Cole Taylor and Jacques Tremaine, but Tremaine was Harold's employer, and Harold could not be mixed up in any business calling for the services of a gang of toughs.

It took a few minutes to retrieve Cole's horse and buggy. Left untied, the nervous animal had bolted down a side street, not stopping until it had found an open garden gate. There it had come to an awkward halt with one buggy wheel wedged into the gate but within reach of a row of carefully tended tomato plants.

By the time Cole had untangled the vehicle, pulled the reluctant horse from the garden, and paid the owner for the razing of her tomato crop, he was decidedly out of temper. Probably if it had not been for the trembling Chinese girl on the seat between them, he would have given Marianna a thorough scolding then and there. Instead, he merely glared at her and began talking to Mi Ling in Chinese.

Feeling somewhat left out, Marianna pretended a sudden interest in their surroundings. But her mind was active with questions. Why had those men accosted Mi Ling? She had no money, nothing valuable in the package she continued to hold so tightly; in fact, Marianna suspected the contents were nothing more than her own cotton petticoat and chemise.

Guided apparently by Mi Ling's instructions, Cole was taking them to Chinatown. Marianna could not help feeling a little triumphant as she realized she was getting her wish to visit this exotic section of the city after all.

It was unlike any place she had ever seen. The colors of the buildings were vivid reds and blues and greens, lavishly trimmed with yellow or gold. Instead of the usual brick or stone fronts, elaborate façades were cut out and painted to look like pagodas. Strings of Chinese paper lanterns brightened the store windows. Colorful signs, decorated with peacocks and fierce-looking dragons, hung out over the street, vying for the passer-by's attention.

Catching Marianna's eye, Cole started a rueful smile, then winced as a sharp pain reminded him of the cut under his eye.

"As exciting as you expected?" he asked over Mi Ling's bent head.

"Better," Marianna told him honestly, not able to resist the fascination of the adventure at the same time that she worried about her frightened friend and the angry bruises that had begun to swell on Cole's face and hands.

Theirs seemed to be the only horse-drawn vehicle on the street. The wealthy inhabitants of Chinatown preferred the human-drawn rickshaw and the poor relied upon their own feet. Marianna spotted a few pedestrians clothed in rich Mandarin costumes, gleaming with costly silk and gold thread embroidery. But most of the people wore the same almost shapeless dark pants and tunic as Mi Ling. With their heads bowed and identical black pigtails flowing down their backs, it was impossible to distinguish men from women.

She did see a sumptuously clad woman step from a rickshaw near a gaudy house that looked like a three-tiered Oriental wedding cake. Marianna felt a moment of envy at the long, form-fitting silk dress heavily encrusted with what looked like gold dragons. The woman's hair had been piled atop her head in an elaborate style, and her face would have been breathtakingly beautiful without the heavy cosmetics visible even from a distance.

"Celestials," Cole had called the people of Chinatown and the name had puzzled Marianna. Now she understood, for seen away from the American city in their own exotic setting, the Chinese reminded her of the sky at midnight—dark and mysterious and clad with stars.

Mi Ling's home was two rooms over a busy Chinese laundry. Her father and three brothers ran the laundry, and looking at the steaming caldrons and heating irons, Marianna shuddered a little. Yet for all the moist atmosphere and hectic activity, the laundry was spotlessly clean. Even the bare board floors, damp from the constant splashing of water and dripping of wet clothes, looked as though they had been freshly scrubbed.

Mi Ling explained the presence of the two Americans to her father with downcast eyes and trembling accents. Remembering the girl's tendency to blame herself, Marianna wondered if she were apologizing for having somehow caused the attack.

The old man—his snow-white queue rather than his face proclaiming his age—listened courteously but silently. Marianna imagined sorrow in his eyes; yet the somber set of his face did not change, and the only physical expression of compassion or concern was a brief touch on his daughter's bent head. Nonetheless, he smiled broadly as he urged Cole and Marianna to join him upstairs for tea.

"We have only a brief home here but it is yours," he assured them.

Puzzled by the expression "brief home," Marianna turned to Mi Ling and was surprised to learn that not only did the family still consider China to be home but also Mi Ling's mother and six other brothers and sisters had already returned there.

"When we have earned the money for our passage, we will also return," Mi Ling told her solemnly, and after the incident in the San Francisco streets, Marianna could well understand the family's desire to leave.

The temporary home was, as Marianna expected, too small for five people; she had not expected, however, the gracious, homelike atmosphere, comfortable in spite of the size and attractive in spite of the location over a steaming laundry.

Silk wall hangings softened the room, and delicate screens painted with Oriental landscapes dimmed the harsh afternoon light. Low chairs and a comfortable looking ottoman were covered with needlework of exquisite delicacy. A soft crimson carpet featured an intricate pattern in which red and gold dragons mingled with red and white pagodas. In the center of the carpet sat a heavily lacquered tea table, inlaid with mother-of-pearl peacocks.

"Tea will be ready shortly," Mi Ling told them. Then she added with a little smile, "Always there is plenty of hot water in a laundry."

First, though, she brought a basin that smelled delicately of herbs and offered it with soft cloths and a little jar of salve to Marianna for tending Cole Taylor's injuries.

Blushing at the girl's obvious assumption that Cole Taylor somehow belonged to her and that, therefore, she would wish to care for him herself, Marianna nonetheless accepted the basin.

"Are you sure you can handle this?" Cole asked with a twinkle in his eyes that said clearly he had noticed her blush and understood the cause.

"I have helped my sister—a nurse—many times in her *animal* hospital," Marianna told him mischievously. "That should more than qualify me to take care of you."

The treatment did help. The herbs soothed the heated skin where the bruised tissues had swelled and stretched while an ingredient in the salve numbed the pain.

Then while Marianna and Mi Ling discussed needlework—a craft in which they discovered a shared interest—Cole and Mi Ling's father spoke in low tones. When they finally rose from the tea table, Marianna thought she saw a paper exchange hands, and Cole slipped something unobtrusively into an inner pocket of his coat.

"What was that all about?" she asked him as soon as their host had bowed them through the front door of the laundry.

Cole climbed into the buggy and used his uninjured hand to pull Marianna up after him. With his hat tipped toward the back of his head, his hair tousled carelessly over his forehead, and the bruise on his cheek coloring alarmingly, he looked impudent and rather guilty.

"You won't like it," he admitted finally, with the little half grin that had begun to exasperate Marianna.

"I insist you tell me about it," she began, adding as an afterthought, "and explain exactly how what you have done involves me. That lovely old man bowed over my hand when we left as though he were thanking me for saving his life. I know it has something to do with that paper you have hidden in your pocket."

For an answer Cole reached into his pocket, took out the paper, and handed it to Marianna. The document appeared to be a legal contract involving the Celestials; however, its import eluded her. Moreover, she noticed her own name occupied a prominent place next to the signatures of Cole and Mi Ling's father.

"To put it simply, I bought her for you."

"You what?"

Cole looked at her somewhat sheepishly from the corner of his eye, but he avoided facing her, making a great show instead of guiding his horse through an intersection blocked by an overturned lumber wagon.

"It's not like she's a slave . . . more like an indentured servant," he explained hastily. "And you won't have to do anything unless the people Mi Ling's father owes money to try again to take her as payment."

Marianna was stunned. "You mean those men were actually trying to take Mi Ling in payment for her father's debt?"

Cole nodded grimly. "Happens all the time. A Chinese family is recruited by agents to come to San Francisco. The agents pay the passage; then when the family gets here, they ask for their money. If the family can't pay—and most can't—the agents take a son or a daughter in exchange.

"Now if the agents come for Mi Ling, her father can say she belongs to an American lady."

It was a neat solution, Marianna had to admit, but how she would explain her having a Chinese slave—it amounted to the same thing, no matter what Cole said—to her aunt and, worse yet, to her father, who was a charter member of the Philadelphia Society for the Abolition of Slavery, Marianna had no idea.

She was thoroughly exhausted emotionally as well as physically by the time they reached the hotel. Wanting nothing more than to hide in her room, she gave Cole a wan smile and had started to climb from the buggy when he caught her hand in his.

"You do understand now why I said you should return to Philadelphia, don't you? Someday San Francisco will be a fit place for ladies to live but not now. Go home, Marianna, and go home soon."

She flung his hand away as though it had burned her; then, not caring about the curious looks of passersby, she stormed at him, "You are unbelievable. You trick me into seeing you behind my fiancé's back. You say you care for me and . . . and you kiss me. Then you involve me in a street brawl, buy me—me! the daughter of a Philadelphia clergyman—a slave, and you say, 'Now go home, Marianna,' just like that." The facts that he had not found it necessary to trick her into seeing him, and that *she* had actually involved *him* in the brawl seemed incidental.

"Well, let me tell you this, Cole Taylor. I will go home when I am good and ready."

If she had glanced over her shoulder as she flounced up the broad stairs to the hotel, Marianna would have seen a broad grin spread over Cole Taylor's face in spite of the aching bruise on his cheek. Then he cocked his hat jauntily to one side of his head and drove away whistling.

Inside the lobby a stately grandfather clock chimed the quarter-hour: "One forty-five." Marianna noted the time and could hardly believe the events of the past four short hours.

By now, of course, her aunt would have read her note. She would be fortunate indeed if half of the city were not out looking for her.

To her amazement, Aunt Myriah seemed neither alarmed nor concerned. As Marianna entered the suite, a luncheon was being laid out on the balcony overlooking the garden. Her aunt greeted her with an offhand wave and a critical look and comment, all directed toward Marianna's hair. "You're making a mistake, my dear, not to do something about those curls. They will positively kink in this damp coast atmosphere."

Several minutes passed before Marianna realized that, far from being worried about her, the older woman had heartily approved of her absence. Assuming that the "business" mentioned in her niece's note had been the glamorizing make-over she had decided on the night before, Aunt Myriah had even expected her to be gone longer.

Marianna had no chance to try to explain the real reasons for her absence, for they were interrupted by a thunderous knocking at the door. Harold strode in, demanding, "What's this I hear about you starting a brawl in the streets and involving Mr. Tremaine in the battle?"

The resulting explanations took them late into the afternoon. Finally finished with trying to justify her actions, Marianna found her way to the safe haven of her bedroom. Aunt Myriah seemed to be under the impression that Marianna had encountered Cole Taylor and the Chinese maid on her way to a fashionable modiste, while Harold, most annoyed that she had somehow involved his boss in an escapade, believed she had gone riding with Jacques Tremaine. Marianna was too tired to explain any more and too tired also to put up with the pair's fury if they fully understood the extent of her morning's folly.

In her absence the room had been straightened and her trunk unpacked. Marianna thought she recognized Mi Ling's delicate hand in the graceful arrangement of fresh flowers on the dressing table and the homelike positioning of her things around the room—her robe on a chair and her slippers beside it, ready to slip into; her vanity case and combs on the dressing table; her Bible and writing desk on the table beside the bed.

Undressing quickly, Marianna donned the robe and, throwing back the quilted coverlet, climbed onto the bed. For an instant she hesitated, then reached out and picked up the Bible. It was old and worn, thumbed and underlined thoroughly from cover to cover. From an early age all the Windemeres had had instilled within them the habit of daily Bible reading. "Read until you find something that touches your heart and answers whatever need is most pressing for the day," their father had always said. And for years Marianna had faithfully gone to the Word for her daily spiritual food. But not lately. She seemed to have gotten out of the habit. In the morning she was rushed; during the day she was not at home; at night she was too sleepy.

And lately, too, she seemed to have gotten out of the habit of going to the Lord with her daily problems. She had not stopped praying—far from it; she bombarded heaven daily with her petitions. But she always seemed to be telling God what she wanted rather than asking what he wanted for her.

Is that what's really wrong with me? Am I in the wrong place at the wrong time because I put myself here? The notion was frightening. How would she get out of the tangles her own self-will had gotten her into? She was

2,500 miles from home, so she could not go to her parents for help. Her Aunt Myriah was interested only in furthering her schemes for Harold.

"No one can help me now but you, Lord," she told him humbly. Then she remembered one of her favorite verses in Romans 8. Leafing quickly through the pages, she found the words heavily underlined and starred to remind her of their importance: "For I am persuaded, that neither death, nor life, nor angels, nor principalities, nor powers, nor things present, nor things to come, nor height, nor depth, nor any other creature, shall be able to separate us from the love of God, which is in Christ Jesus our Lord."

CHAPTER 5

San Francisco
Sunday, July 2, 1855

Dear Gloriana,

The Yankee Clipper *sails today, and Aunt Myriah and I will not be on it. We have taken a smallish house on one of the narrow, climbing streets—small because even Aunt Myriah's comfortable purse cannot stand the San Francisco prices long.*

The cost of living here is unbelievable. Single rooms at our hotel were $37.50 a week, and our suite was over $100. The price of a single meal in the hotel restaurant would feed a family back East for a month. Sourdough bread—the staple of San Franciscans' diet—sells for $1.00 a loaf, and a loaf of yeast-raised white bread may bring as high as $3.00, probably because it reminds these homesick Californians of home. I have heard that in the winter the price of a dozen eggs may run as much as $4.60, and fresh milk is priceless.

Why we are setting up housekeeping in this gold-crazed city can be explained in one word—Harold. He won't go home, and Aunt Myriah won't go home without him.

Marianna paused in her writing and, chewing thoughtfully on the tip of the pencil, recalled the events of the past few days—the showdown between mother and son, Aunt Myriah's decision to stay in San Francisco, the search for a house. Her aunt had at first considered buying, but with empty lots going for $5,000 a quarter acre, and tar-paper shacks for $12,000, she could not. Marianna smiled a little at the thought of her well-to-do aunt's finding it necessary to economize. To the often purse-pinched Windemeres, the Von Wootens had seemed wealthy. *But out here wealth is measured in millions of dollars and tons of gold,* Marianna thought, wondering at the difference a few thousand miles could make. *We're not in a different country. California is a full-fledged part of the United States. But we are in a different world.* Then she resumed writing.

I can't say I am unhappy with her decision. Don't get me wrong, my romantic sister. I am not catching the western fever, and I certainly could never marry one of these wild western men, though I'm sure your own "wild man" is perfectly marvelous. Unfortunately, the ones I have met would not rate as matrimonial prizes.

First, there's Cole Taylor. He's a giant, of course, with dark curly hair; a face somewhat worse for the battering of a hundred fist fights; and an arrogant, king-of-the-hill manner. He is, I have been told, an alderman of this fair city and the founder of the '49ers Volunteer Fire-Fighting Club, not to mention the owner of various steamships, warehouses, and stores. I don't like him, but there's no need to go into that.

Next Harold's elegant employer comes to mind—and I do mean elegant. *Jacques Tremaine is as handsome as a lord in one of those Jane Austen novels we used to sigh over as little girls. He dresses all in black, speaks with a French accent, and has the most sinister eyes; they make my heart leap right into my throat every time he looks at me.*

Harold, of course, does not rate as a westerner yet, though he is trying very hard to fit in. He copies

Jacques Tremaine's dress and romantic manner and is developing Cole Taylor's annoying habit of arranging other people's lives for them. Harold is not at all pleased with our staying here, but he can't do much about it. You know Aunt Myriah.

Sister-mine, it hurts to be so close to you and yet still so far away. How I long to see you and the babies, not to mention my one-and-only brother-in-law.

Remember me often in your prayers.

Your loving sister,
Marianna Windemere

After signing her name with a flourish, Marianna folded the letter quickly and hastily addressed an envelope to "Mrs. Graham Norton, Applegate Landing, Oregon Territory." The address seemed woefully inadequate without a street or box number.

Moreover, she felt rather childish writing in pencil rather than ink, though her sister had often assured the family that pencil was better for a letter sent into the wilderness. The lead would not run, but ink might if the mail should happen to get wet. Marianna laughed as she tried to imagine how a pouch of U. S. mail might "happen to get wet." It was little short of incredible that she could send a piece of paper into the wilderness with only the name of some remote frontier village as direction and expect it to reach its destination.

"But this is one time the mail had better get through," she said, thinking of the sizeable bite the postage for this letter and the one she was sending back home was taking out of her spending money, not to mention the cost of sending a neighbor boy to the docks to post them. Errand boys did not come cheap in a town where miners on holiday handed out gold nuggets as tips.

They also tend toward impatience, Marianna realized as she heard a shrill whistle at the front gate. A fistful of letters already in his hand and, Marianna had no doubt, a pocket full of silver dollars, the boy sat poised on his velocipede, ready to race toward the dock.

"I'll make it for sure before the *Yankee Clipper* sails,"

he promised Marianna, then pulled his flat cap down firmly over his ears, and raced down the unpaved hilly street at a pace that took her breath away.

From her vantage point near the hilltop, Marianna had a clear view of the harbor. Soon the *Yankee Clipper* would be riding across the velvety blue expanse, its white canvas sails filled with the wind, its deck rolling on the swells. The thought made her achingly homesick. At least three months would pass before the familiar clipper reached the East Coast; another three or four before it could return. Other ships would be sailing, of course; the harbor was filled with them. But somehow the *Yankee Clipper*'s sailing without her left Marianna feeling stranded, as though she might never see home again.

"Better take a different tack," she scolded herself, falling unconsciously into nautical cant as she brushed angrily at her wet eyelashes. "Think instead about those letters. The penciled one to Gloriana will sail north to Eureka, then go overland on the Jacksonville Trail." How delightful it would be to travel that same route. She would love to see Eureka. The name from the Greek for "I found it!" fascinated her. She had noticed it embossed on the state seal with a miner wielding a pickax in the background and supposed it meant the town was the site of another gold strike.

The other letter, more elegantly penned in ink, would be at sea for months, rounding the Horn in the southern hemisphere's worst winter storms and perhaps, if the trade winds were good, reaching New York around the first week in October. She tried not to imagine her family's reaction when they realized she was not aboard.

"Plan a bridal shower for November and the wedding for Christmas," she had told them confidently. At least staying here would save her the embarrassment of going back alone, a jilted bride.

In the meantime she and her aunt would be more than comfortable in their hilltop cottage. A compact two stories, the house perched rather than sat in a narrow terraced garden. Scalloped siding, painted a cheery yellow, covered the sides as well as a rounded tower that peaked in a witch's-hat-roof above the second floor. Creamy white trim, lathed and carved into an intricate gingerbread of spools and swirls, edged the roof and windows and matched the railing of the porch that surrounded the front and one side of the first floor.

From a second-floor window Mi Ling leaned to shake the dust from her mop and, seeing Marianna at the gate, waved happily. Aunt Myriah had been thrilled to find a maid willing to work at any wage and had not questioned the $40 a month figure Marianna had cited. Mi Ling, for her part, had been reluctant to accept a salary, insisting she owed Marianna her services, and had only given in after Marianna had pointed out how far the money would go toward purchasing passage to China.

Hiring Mi Ling had provided a short-term solution to her problem. Looking at the maid's bright smile and glowing face beneath its glossy fringe of bangs, Marianna had strong hopes for a long-term solution. The Chinese truck gardener who delivered produce door-to-door on their street had visited the house daily since they had moved in, and Marianna had surprised more than one appreciative glance following the thick black braid that hung provocatively to Mi Ling's slim hips.

"You're looking very pleased with yourself." Harold had come through the garden gate while Marianna was admiring her temporary home. The grayish tint of his face and the great circles under his eyes showed the hazard of mixing a late Saturday night with a commitment to attend Sunday morning church services.

"Shouldn't I be?" she challenged gaily and twirled so that he could receive the full effect of her hoop-skirted, ivory-colored frock. The flowers appliquéd in the same shade on the sleeves and around the stand-out hem added detail without ruining the classic lines, and a wide band of creamy velvet ribbon, passing under the bodice to tie in a large bow with trailing streamers at her back, provided a coyly flirtatious finishing touch.

"If you're pleased with the way you look, you have every right to be. If you're pleased not to be on that ship getting ready to sail from the harbor, that's another matter."

The smile on Marianna's face disappeared instantly. "If you're still complaining about our being in San Francisco, you had better talk to your stepmother. I have nothing more to say to you on the subject." And to emphasize the point, she turned and ran up the long wooden steps that climbed from the street to the porch. "Running away from bossy males is getting to be a habit with you," Marianna told herself disapprovingly. She did not need to look to visualize the scowl on Harold's face as he followed her; in fact, she could see to the last detail his furrowed forehead and his grimacing mouth as he chewed angrily on a drooping edge of his mustache.

The other bossy male in her life had been strangely invisible since their adventure into Chinatown. Mi Ling had told her he had called at her father's laundry and arranged to have the linens at the club where he lived washed weekly. He had been mentioned in a newspaper article as one of the officials at a boxing match. But she had neither seen nor heard from Cole Taylor. *We move in different circles,* she had concluded, with a disdainful sniff at his imagined low pursuits.

Consequently, she was not at all prepared to see him in church, sharing a hymn book with a red-haired beauty.

"Marianna, isn't that person in the third row that awful Cole Taylor?" Aunt Myriah's whisper had a remarkable carrying power, and Marianna colored in embarrassment as heads, including Cole's, turned in their direction. She pretended not to see his smiling nod, but she could not miss Harold's envious, "Not only is that Taylor, but he has Christina Dowling, the richest widow in San Francisco, with him."

The beautiful church should have lifted Marianna's spirits and helped her send her thoughts heavenward. Three long rows of polished pews bordered aisles with thick red carpeting. Sunlight streamed through stained-glass windows set deep in stone arches along the walls. A giant circle of hundreds of lead-framed pieces of glass, shaped in the classic rose pattern of red and green and gold, was positioned like a window to heaven high above the altar. The organ music was deep and mellow; the hymns, familiar and joyous.

But Marianna's eyes kept straying to Cole's dark head, looking uncharacteristically bare without his usual low-crowned black hat, tipped back over tousled curls.

She wished to be able to slip out quickly after the service, but Aunt Myriah lingered, shaking hands and becoming acquainted with the churchgoers. Harold, sticking his hands in his pockets, stood staring rudely at the people and looking bored.

"Miss Windemere, may I present Mrs. Dowling?" The by-now familiar deep voice started a chill somewhere in the area of her heart, but Marianna managed a bright smile as she acknowledged the introduction. The widow was stunning and young—under twenty-five by Marianna's guess. Her expensive black crepe tailored mourning dress showed her loss was recent. The stark color, unrelieved by any lighter accents, would have made most redheads look washed out and drab, but the contrast only served to heighten the glowing whiteness of Christina Dowling's skin and the tropically vivid combination of green eyes, black brows and lashes, and rosy lips and cheeks.

"I am very happy to meet you, Marianna. May I call you that? Cole has talked of you so much, I feel we are old friends. I hope you will visit me soon."

Unable to think of any courteous refusal, Marianna stammered something she hoped to be noncommittal. She sensed Cole looking at her questioningly, and to cover her confusion, turned and, pulling Harold forward, introduced him as her fiancé.

Mrs. Dowling glanced curiously at Cole. His bland expression apparently told her nothing, for she quickly included Harold in an invitation for a Fourth of July celebration.

"I wish you hadn't accepted for us without asking me," Marianna told Harold crankily as they left the church.

"Why? You seemed taken with her. I haven't seen you smile so much since you landed here. I thought you would want to start getting to know people. Besides, it's not every day one has the chance to get acquainted with someone as rich as Christina Dowling."

Marianna had no answer for that. Why it was so important to Harold to be acquainted with rich people she had no idea. She knew his thoughtlessness had committed her to a very uncomfortable day and she would not soon forget it. She did not, however, probe the reasons for her discomfort and carefully avoided, even in her thoughts, any mention of Cole Taylor.

They reached home in time to watch the *Yankee Clipper* make its stately way toward the Golden Gate. Its masts were hung with gleaming white canvas and from their hilltop it looked as though the ship were leaning away from the wind at a forty-degree angle.

Both Harold and Aunt Myriah watched the ship's progress grimly, but neither said a word, as though having reached a tacit agreement that too much had been said already. But Marianna felt again a sharp panic at being left behind.

Seeing her pallor and the tears welling in her eyes, Harold moved closer to put his arm around her. "I know it's not your fault," he whispered. "I don't blame you." And for the first time since she had arrived in San Francisco, Marianna found his presence comforting.

Dinner was a somber affair, served in the tiny dining room just off the kitchen. No one had much to say, and although Mi Ling had prepared the chicken and dumplings perfectly with the tender meat falling apart and the biscuit dough white and fluffy, no one had much of an appetite.

Aunt Myriah refused dessert and excused herself to take a nap. Marianna, however, did not want to hurt Mi Ling's feelings after her struggles over making apple brown betty in the best New England manner, so she stayed.

"You really feel bad about not going, don't you?" Harold questioned her when his stepmother had left the room.

"It's more than that," Marianna admitted. "I have this strange feeling I have taken some irrevocable step that will change my life forever, and there's no turning back."

"Since you feel that way, I'm wondering why you didn't go back alone. You didn't have to let Myriah persuade you to stay here."

He was right. She could have traveled alone, as her sister Gloriana had on her way to Oregon, and Marianna's trip home would have been easier because she would not have been sailing into the unknown wilderness. So why hadn't she?

"I'll tell you what I think," Harold said, his intent gaze never leaving her face. "I think you stayed because of me, because you knew if we were together long enough, everything between us would fall back into place, and you were right."

Harold left his place at the table and came around to Marianna's side to take her unresisting hand.

"I know I'm doing this badly, but what I'm trying to say is since you're here and you're going to be here for quite a while, why don't we go ahead and get married? We are going to do it someday anyway. Why not now?"

Marianna realized suddenly that this was not at all what she wanted at that moment. Marrying Harold Von Wooten, her cousin and playmate, back in the familiar environment of her Philadelphia home had been one thing. Marrying this changed Harold in San Francisco was something else altogether.

"I'll have to think about it," she managed to tell him, but she knew from now on all her aunt's and cousin's considerable powers of persuasion would be bent toward making her say yes.

If I don't want to say yes, why didn't I go home? she kept asking herself over and over during the rest of the day. The answer was easily found but not easily admitted. Only when night had fallen and she was alone at her bedroom window would she allow herself to breathe the secret: she had stayed because of Cole Taylor.

All her anger and loathing had been camouflage to hide her attraction to him. But now he was interested in someone else and she would be pushed into marrying Harold.

From somewhere in the recesses of her mind came the fragment of a poem her father had often recited:

There is a time we know not when,
A place we know not where,
That marks the destiny of men,
To glory or despair.
There is a line by us unseen
That crosses every path,
The hidden boundary between
God's mercy and his wrath.
There is a tide in the affairs of men,
Which taken at the flood leads on to fortune,
Omitted, all the voyage of their lives,
Is bound in shallows and miseries.

Had her chance for happiness sailed with the *Yankee Clipper*? Watching the silver-streaked bay gleaming in the moonlight, Marianna could still see in her mind's eye the tall ship sailing grandly out to sea.

"Dear God, what should I do now?" She sent her petition into the star-filled sky. Vaguely she hoped for a flashing insight telling her to sail on the next ship or even go north to Oregon—anything to get her away from San Francisco. But no insights or traveling orders came.

Then she remembered another of her father's favorite sayings, "When you're at the end of your rope and your prayer seems to go unanswered, wait."

CHAPTER 6

"WAIT ON THE LORD: be of good courage, and he shall strengthen thine heart."

Marianna had need of courage and a stout heart as the Fourth of July dawned clear and sunny. She had prayed earnestly for rain, but the day was the most glorious she had yet seen in San Francisco. The sky was a bright, sun-washed blue; the bay, calm and glowing; the wind, no more than a breeze.

"Couldn't we at least have had fog?" Marianna grumbled heavenward as she waited on the porch for Christina Dowling's carriage. Except for the pout on her face, she presented a festive Fourth of July picture. Her dotted swiss gown was a deep navy blue sprinkled with white. With her white hat trimmed with a bow of wide red grosgrain ribbon and matching red gloves and reticule, she looked appropriately patriotic and, if she had only known it, remarkably pretty.

Usually on the Fourth of July Marianna was eager to be up and going, ready to wait an hour or more as long as she had a good spot on the parade route. Today, though, she was dragging, and an hour late would have been too early for her.

Aunt Myriah had left already to spend the day with an

acquaintance from church. Her letters of introduction had led her unerringly to a circle of kindred spirits, and soon her days would be filled with meetings of the Ladies Aid Society, the Temperance Committee, and various other groups dedicated to missions, charity, and reform. From what Marianna had seen of similar groups back home, their activities would consist primarily of tea and talk.

"If San Francisco were my home, I would start a reforming campaign in earnest," Marianna frowned, remembering again the El Dorado Casino and City Hall, standing side by side.

"Didn't I say the reforming impulse would strike you eventually?"

Startled, Marianna looked up into Cole Taylor's laughing brown eyes.

"If those flowers are any indication, I would say your reforms would involve some rather violent measures." He pointed to the petals of the pink cabbage roses she had been unconsciously decapitating while she thought.

"Violence isn't the answer," she told him seriously as she stood brushing the crushed petals from her lap and avoiding his teasing gaze.

"The vigilantes think so. They'll be out in force today marching in the name of law and order."

"But is it law and order if private citizens have to dispense justice with their own hands?"

Cole looked at her curiously, apparently trying to gauge her mood. "Then what's the answer?"

Marianna hesitated no more than a second. "Families and churches," she said decidedly. "San Francisco won't be reformed until it has as many churches as saloons and dance halls, and until more wives and mothers demand a decent environment in which to bring up their children."

Cole was sitting on the porch rail, his hands in his pockets and his hat, as usual, tipped back casually on his head. His eyes did not leave her face. "Is that why you stayed," he asked quietly, "to become a wife and mother?"

Marianna didn't wish to answer that question, particularly for Cole Taylor, and deliberately ignoring it, she asked a question of her own. "What are you doing here?"

Her challenging tone with its barely concealed note of annoyance brought the grin back to Cole's face.

"I came to collect you for Christina's party." He pointed with a flourish toward the familiar buggy waiting at the gate. His horse, ever the one to seize an opportunity, was leaning over the fence and rapidly devouring a bed of sunny yellow daisies. "I convinced Christina your street is too steep and narrow for her carriage. She went on ahead to pick up *your Harold*." He whistled happily, in spite of Marianna's frowning silence, all the way into the heart of the city.

The streets were crowded with boisterous merrymakers. Many, not content to wait patiently on the sidelines, streamed down the avenues. Christina Dowling had arranged for her guests to watch from a balcony overlooking the intersection of Montgomery and California Streets.

"Owns the building," Harold whispered when Marianna joined them. He didn't seem to notice or care that she had arrived with Cole Taylor.

The party was small. In addition to Marianna and Harold, only two other couples, both middle-aged and bearing the unmistakable stamp of Eastern society, plus three preschool-aged children, Marianna assumed were Mrs. Dowling's, were in attendance.

"The children love parades," her hostess confided, "but I wouldn't dare bring them if we didn't have this place to watch from. Crowds tend to get out of hand in San Francisco."

Watching the turmoil below the balcony, Marianna could well believe it. The boardwalks on each side of the avenue were crammed with people, all jostling each other for a better view. From Marianna's vantage point, she could see a sea of bobbing hats and shoulders, with an occasional brightly colored bonnet or scarf standing out bravely amid the predominant blacks, browns, and sandy beiges. One eager youngster had climbed part way up the pole of a street lamp where he hung precariously peering down the avenue. Several enterprising parade watchers had brought boxes to stand on only to have them pulled abruptly from beneath their feet when they blocked the view of those behind.

A brief hush preceded the first pulsing strains of an oom-pah-pah band drifting down Montgomery Street. Then someone shouted, "They're coming!" And a cheer went up.

Leading the way was a party whose wide banner proclaimed them to be "'49ers." Pickaxes over their shoulders, outsized dungarees held in place by suspenders, hip-length boots, knotted kerchiefs, and floppy hats—their costumes matched to the last detail the daguerreotypes of the gold rush vanguard that had appeared in Eastern papers. On their shoulders several of the miners carried what looked like an irregularly shaped rock, but the crowd's roar of approval suggested something more important.

"The Carson nugget," Harold answered Marianna's question, "195 pounds and the largest nugget ever found in the United States." His voice registered excitement to match the crowd's, but Marianna felt vaguely disappointed. From her vantage point the nugget looked a dirty yellow brown and not particularly large. Apparently the picture in her mind's eye of California bonanzas made up of gleaming golden boulders was a gross exaggeration.

The miners were followed by Spanish dancers. Their sparkling costumes, gleaming with silver and gold embroidery, were reminders of the state's Spanish heritage and its ties, geographical as well as historical, to Mexico on the south. Then came a tribe of Indians, resplendent in feathers and beaded buckskins; cowboys doing rope tricks on the backs of dancing ponies; and always the bands. A fife-and-drum corps passed playing the inevitable "Yankee Doodle." Several oom-pah-pah bands pounded out tunes that all sounded more or less alike. The skirling measures and colorful kilts of Scottish bagpipers, however, went unappreciated by some of the crowd who shouted, "Quit that caterwauling" or "Leave the skirts to the women folk."

Caught up in the excitement, Marianna applauded the marchers and laughed at the antics of a bear, included to represent California's brief identity ten years before as the Bear Flag Republic. Even a marching company of vigilantes drew a smile; the men looked so solemn and impressed with themselves, wearing their pseudomilitary uniforms and following their gold-tasseled crimson banner.

But when the last marcher had passed, Marianna still peered down the street.

"Did you miss something?" Cole had found his way to her side while Harold devoted himself to their hostess.

"Well, yes," Marianna answered vaguely, "I guess I was looking for the dragon. Mi Ling said there would be a Chinese dragon and firecrackers."

"She must have meant a parade in Chinatown. The Celestials have their own way of celebrating holidays."

"Is there another parade?" Christina Dowling, whose enjoyment of the event had been nearly as exuberant as her children's, broke in excitedly. "We can't miss the dragon!"

Marianna had no doubt that if she had suggested going, both Cole Taylor and Harold would have refused, citing unruly crowds and other phantom dangers as reasons. Cole did protest briefly, but he was swiftly overruled by both their hostess and her offspring.

If the keynote for the uptown celebration had been struck by the '49ers and the oom-pah-pah bands, firecrackers and the dragon dominated Chinatown's. The air over the narrow streets sizzled as long strings of firecrackers hanging from upper story windows went off in crackling chain reactions.

"Hold onto my arm," Cole shouted in Marianna's ear to be heard over the din. Remembering her determination to stick close to her fiancé, Marianna looked around for Harold; however, he was occupied—surprisingly since Harold had never liked children—with helping the widow Dowling keep track of her excited youngsters in the crowd.

"Now you have no excuse." Cole's words showed clearly that he had been following her thought processes. Reluctantly she laid her fingers on his sleeve, but he drew her hand through his arm and pressed it tightly to his side.

She was glad, though, of his support a minute later when some pranksters threw a string of firecrackers on the sidewalk at her feet. The tiny red cylinders writhed and sparked with each pop, like a vicious, noisy snake, and Marianna found herself jumping nervously even after Cole had swung her safely out of the way.

"I hate to think of the fires that may get started before today is over," she yelled with a laugh that bordered on the hysterical.

"We firefighters will be busy tonight," he replied and tightened his hold on her reassuringly.

It had been amazing to Marianna that a city the size of San Francisco had no public fire department but relied completely on the efforts of volunteer groups like Cole Taylor's '49ers. Now she wondered about the dedication and civic spirit that must be involved in volunteering to fight fires in narrow streets lined with towering wooden buildings. Obvious firetraps, she realized, trying not to think about the people who might lose their homes and the firefighters who might lose their lives in Chinatown.

Crashing cymbals and a metallic roar, like someone shaking a huge metal sheet, signaled the approach of the dragon. Having imagined a huge but immovable creature made perhaps of papier-mâché and drawn on rollers, Marianna was completely unprepared for the moving, breathing dragon. Smoke belched from its open red mouth. Its eyes rolled threateningly and its undulating green tail stretched for a block or more, moving on quick, stamping feet.

Spellbound, she watched breathlessly as the dragon left the street and chased a group of spectators along the sidewalk. Its long tongue lashed out absurdly and puffs of smoke covered the victims.

A portion of the tail lifted just long enough to reveal a face. Marianna caught her breath as she recognized the man as one of Mi Ling's attackers, and in the next second she realized the thing pointing in their direction was a gun.

Not stopping to think, she shoved a bewildered Cole back into the crowd. Exploding firecrackers covered the report of the gun, and for a second it looked as though her overheated imagination had been playing tricks on her. Then a spectator, a Chinese man who had been standing close beside them, collapsed, a red stain covering the front of his tunic.

"That was meant for you," Marianna shouted as she frantically held onto Cole. The noise of the celebration kept knowledge of the tragedy from spreading as bystanders rushed to assist the wounded man. Eerily the parade went on; the undulating dragon tail continued to weave from one side of the street to the other; and the firecrackers and cymbals blended with the sounds of bells and shouting voices in a deafening cacophony of sound.

The image of that harsh face—its sharply hooked nose set over a scowling mouth and square, jutting jawline—and the long blue barrel of the gun stayed with Marianna throughout the rest of that day. Cole had insisted she say nothing about the incident to their hostess. "The man who was killed was probably some wealthy merchant who refused to pay protection money. Assassinations like that happen everyday in Chinatown." And he had dismissed the idea that the shot was meant for him from discussion. "Beating someone in a fair fight is not a motive for murder."

But Marianna could not dismiss it from her mind so easily. *The men who had tried to abduct Mi Ling had been working for someone. Could that someone want Cole Taylor out of the way?*

Cole, however, joked through an elegant patio luncheon at Christina Dowling's Park Place mansion. The Mediterranean-style house and grounds—all marble and fountains and ornate balustrades—oppressed Marianna with their heavy-handed grandeur, but Cole seemed perfectly at home.

Probably from long acquaintance, Marianna thought resentfully, though she knew she had no right to feel that way. Still, Harold was falling over himself with admiring his hostess and all her possessions, and Marianna's status as his fiancée gave her a right to be jealous of him. She nursed that jealousy through an interminable afternoon and evening of listening to political speeches in Union Square, dining at the Astor House, and watching fireworks shot from Pelican Rock out over the bay. When it was finally time to thank her hostess and say good night, she felt like a fraud, smiling prettily and expressing her appreciation, when her thoughts had bordered on the murderous for hours.

"You've been very quiet all day. Still worrying about what happened in Chinatown?" In spite of her assurances that she could walk if the carriage left her at the bottom of the hill, Cole and his buggy had once again been charged with escorting Marianna.

"Why should I be concerned about it if you're not?" Her voice sounded snappish even to Marianna's ears, but she was too tired for ordinary politeness.

Around them in the lamplit darkness the city continued to celebrate, with exploding firecrackers, with music and laughter, some lighthearted and joyous, some raucous and bordering on that quarrelsome state that signals the onset of drunkenness. Through it all the steady clipclopping of the horse's hoofs and the clattering of the buggy wheels on the planked avenues echoed reassuringly.

"Marianna, I want you to know I understand and appreciate what you tried to do today. If you had been right about the gunman, you would have saved my life and I want to thank you. Does it really matter so much what happens to me?"

"Of course it matters. You're a human being like anyone else, and I don't like to see people hurt."

Cole brought the buggy to a stop on a hill overlooking the bay and turned to face her. It was too dark to see the expression in his eyes, but his lips turned up slightly in his familiar half-mocking smile. Remembering the last time they sat together on such a lookout, Marianna moved hastily to the far side of the seat.

"Are you running away from me?" Cole asked with a chuckle.

"I'm . . . I'm just more comfortable over here," she stammered and then felt like kicking herself for letting him once again make her nervous.

A cool breeze stirred the curls that peeked from beneath her bonnet and she shivered, hugging herself tightly.

"You're cold." Cole's voice was light and teasing. He took off his coat and, moving closer, wrapped it snugly around her. "You're right. It is more comfortable over here," he said softly as his hand squeezed her shoulder.

For a moment she thought he was going to kiss her again, and she fought against the overpowering urge to close her eyes. Instead his cheek rested softly against hers, and glancing down at her ungloved hand, she remembered his promise not to kiss her while she wore Harold's ring.

Finally, he cleared his voice of huskiness and, tipping her chin gently, made her meet his eyes. His look was both tender and sincere as he told her softly, "You are one special lady, Marianna Windemere. I'm beginning to think God knew what he was doing when he brought you to San Francisco."

CHAPTER 7

HAD GOD, NOT HER OWN WILLFULNESS brought her to San Francisco? Marianna was not certain. But she could be thankful at least that she had been in Chinatown to push Cole Taylor out of the way of an assassin's bullet and thankful too that she had been on hand when Mi Ling needed her. Whether she were equally thankful for the chance, perhaps even the responsibility, to help Harold Von Wooten, Marianna was uncertain.

In the days since their arrival, her fiancé had blown hot, then cold, then hot again. He had asked her to go home. He had suggested, almost casually, that they marry soon. He had alternately ignored her and heckled her with a fierce jealousy of which she had not known him capable.

Of course, the jealousy was in part her fault, Marianna admitted guiltily. Somehow Harold had finally heard about her trip to Chinatown with Cole and even about her being in his arms on the lookout point the evening of Christina Dowling's Fourth of July party. Harold's reaction had been explosive.

"You are making a fool of me and letting Taylor make a fool of you. Everyone knows he has the inside track with Christina Dowling, and he has practically taken over her business interests since her husband was shot. Some people even say the reason that shooting has never been solved is Taylor doesn't want it to be. The man's an out-and-out scoundrel."

This time Harold had demanded she marry him immediately; this time Marianna had refused. Though her conscience smarted with the knowledge she had indeed been unfair to him, she had no intention of marrying Harold to help him save face. Moreover, she had not missed his unmistakable suggestion that given an inside track with the widowed Mrs. Dowling, no man would possibly choose Marianna Windemere instead.

"You're promised to me, Marianna," he had stormed at her. "I thought you churchy types kept your promises."

"And you promised me a wedding and a home in Philadelphia," Marianna had replied valiantly, though the scene and Harold's anger had brought tears to her eyes and made her tremble with revulsion.

Surprisingly, Aunt Myriah had heartily approved of her stand.

"Don't give in to him," she had said with a reassuring pat on Marianna's hand. "We'll bring that young man to his senses yet. I have a plan."

Relieved that at least this plan did not require her becoming glamorized in the San Francisco fashion, Marianna had dismissed it from her mind until the morning a week later when she found herself accompanying her aunt to the sumptuous Market Street offices of Harold's boss, Jacques Tremaine.

It was a foggy, damp day. Gray wisps curled around them as they descended their hilly side street to Sacramento Avenue, where they could board the horse-drawn streetcar. The mists acted like a cushion to sound, muffling city noises to a murmur. Even the clang-clang of the streetcar and the heavy clopping of its team of Clydesdales were muted.

The car was already full, though they were near the top of Sacramento Avenue with a long, sweeping ride ahead to the wharves and the end of the run. However, two men sprang quickly to their feet and, tipping their hats, offered seats to the ladies.

Certainly living in a city where the population is predominantly male has some advantages, Marianna thought, and she smiled thanks for both herself and her aunt.

Aunt Myriah had adopted her most impressive demeanor and only nodded. A long-time member of what was commonly called the "carriage trade," she rarely used public transportation, and her expression said clearly that her presence on a streetcar was not an invitation to make the acquaintance of either herself or her niece.

Some curious glances were cast in their direction, but for the most part the men in the car were intent upon reading their newspapers and smoking giant cigars whose foul smell hung heavily in the dank air.

The cost of riding the streetcar was fifty cents—two bits apiece with a little nickel-sized token of orange cardboard to allow them to transfer to the Market Street car. The ride would have been worth it at two or three times the price. With straining brakes holding the car in check on the steep incline, they seemed at first to be floating on a cloud; then they plunged into a gray, out-of-focus world where hulking stone buildings looked soft and rounded at the edges and streaming tendrils of fog moved with ghostly purpose.

The atmosphere was perfect for mysteries, and leaning toward her aunt, Marianna whispered a question—speaking loudly seemed somehow inappropriate in the fog—about her plan.

"You'll find out soon enough," her aunt responded shortly, but even she lowered her tone to match the mood of the day.

Market Street was crammed with carriages and pedestrians in spite of the weather. A gloomy half-light blended people and things into a monochromatic collage of gray sky, gray buildings, and gray people.

Tremaine's offices were on the top floor of a palatial building. An enormous chandelier, lighted in spite of the early hour, hung over Brussels carpets in a cavernous lobby.

Ever bothered by her tight shoes and aching feet, Aunt Myriah opted to ride the mechanical lift rather than climb the long flight of stairs that spiraled in an open, echoing tower to the roof. Operated by wheels and pulleys, the lift rose slowly but smoothly upward with only an occasional jerk to remind them of the floors they were passing and the dizzying heights they were scaling.

"Now let me do all the talking," her aunt told Marianna, and the younger woman stifled a nervous giggle. How could she talk when she had no idea what this visit was all about? What kind of plan did Aunt Myriah have for forcing Harold to go home? And what role did she want Jacques Tremaine to play in it?

Whatever she's planning, Harold will be furious with us for involving his employer. Marianna remembered his anger when she had persuaded Mr. Tremaine to aid Cole Taylor in a fist fight. His fury then would probably be a pale imitation of how he would react if he ever found out about today's visit, and stepping off the lift, Marianna looked around furtively, then took a deep breath of relief. Harold at least was nowhere in sight.

What she did see, however, set off alarms in her head. Stepping from an office down the long carpeted hall was the man with the hooked nose and jutting jaw. She gasped. His eyes met hers menacingly; then he slipped back inside.

"What was that, Marianna? Did the lift stop too quickly for you? I always hate that sinking sensation before the wretched thing stops. Makes me feel as though I have swallowed my tongue." The old lady bustled as she pushed her stunned niece toward impressive double doors with the name "Jacques Tremaine, Esquire" in ornate gold letters on the frosted glass.

A bespectacled secretary with a flat brown toupee assured them that they were expected and motioned them to a brocade, French-style settee. Marianna sank to the stiff-looking cushion, glad of a chance to get her trembling limbs under control.

It was he. But how could it have been? Could those men who attacked Mi Ling work for Jacques Tremaine?

But if they did, why had he agreed to help Cole when Marianna appealed to him? She had not seen Tremaine since the day of the fight, but she remembered the mocking amusement in his eyes as clearly as though she were looking into them now. Surely a man like that would not fight his own employees just to play the gallant gentleman for a lady. Besides, if they worked for Mr. Tremaine, what did he want with Mi Ling?

Too bewildered to arrive at any quick answers, Marianna looked up obediently at her aunt's quick nudge. The door to the inner office had opened, revealing Tremaine and a black-clad woman. His dark head was bent over her hand in the gesture Marianna remembered. She suppressed another little gasp and drew a disapproving glare from her aunt as the woman in black turned and Marianna recognized Christina Dowling.

"Mrs. Von Wooten! Marianna!" The widow called their names as though crying for a lifeline. Ordinarily Marianna's feelings for the beautiful Mrs. Dowling were less than charitable, but she recognized the sheer terror in the woman's eyes.

With a smile Marianna stood and extended her hand. The long slim fingers that clasped hers were icy and trembling.

"Congratulate me, ladies," Mrs. Dowling was chattering too gaily. "I have just persuaded one of our city's wealthiest businessmen to contribute $10,000 toward the Chinatown Girls' Shelter."

Marianna looked quickly to Jacques Tremaine and again she saw the look of unholy amusement in his eyes. The day he had answered her appeal to fight, that look had sent shivers down her spine; now it chilled her to the bone.

Impulsively, she gave Christina Dowling's hand a firm squeeze and volunteered her help. "I'm not a wealthy businessman, but surely I can do something."

The support seemed to be exactly what the widow needed. She accepted readily but clung to Marianna's hand while her color returned to normal and her breathing steadied, then with a promise to call on them, hurried through the doors to the lift.

Tremaine, who had been waiting to escort Marianna and her aunt to his office, commented smoothly but somehow sarcastically, "Ah, another lovely lady embarked on good works, precisely what our city needs."

The office, like the rest of the building was palatial. Priceless Persian rugs softened a gleaming hardwood floor. The desk was oriental mahogany, carved intricately and polished to a glass-smooth shine. A fist-sized gold nugget was being used as a paperweight on the otherwise cleared desktop.

"We have come about my stepson," Myriah Von Wooten began as soon as they were seated. "I want you to fire him."

The request, more like an order, startled Marianna, but Jacques Tremaine appeared completely unmoved.

"Why?" he asked, with a what's-in-it-for-me challenge in his voice.

"I am prepared to offer you $20,000 and the deed to a Dakota gold mine."

Marianna caught her breath and stared at her aunt in amazement. The money was probably no more than Tremaine spent at the roulette wheel on a single night. The gold mine was worthless, the only asset of a '49er her uncle had grubstaked, never to see again. When he had investigated the deed, her uncle had been told that the claim was in the Black Hills, a part of Sioux territory protected "in perpetuity" by treaty. The mine was a family joke.

Tremaine arched his eyebrows expressively but made no comment. Instead, he turned to Marianna. "And what about Mademoiselle Windemere?" he asked with just a trace of a sneer in his lightly accented voice. "Is she also anxious to see her fiancé out of employment?"

"No!" Marianna startled herself and her aunt with her answer. "I, of course, want Harold to come home, but I want him to come back of his own free will."

Tremaine's eyes held hers, and Marianna had a fleeting impression he in some amazing way was apprehensive about her. The impression was gone in a moment, but it added another puzzle to those confronting her all morning.

"Is it not true that what one holds freely will often slip away? But perhaps Mademoiselle is no longer so interested in holding this not-so-eager fiancé. Perhaps she has found another, shall we say, more ardent admirer?"

The insinuation brought color to Marianna's cheeks. She knew now the source of Harold's information about her meetings with Cole Taylor.

Seeing her blush and her aunt's equally red flush of anger, Tremaine laughed and stood. "Enough of what you call the cat-and-mouse game. I am sure you dear ladies both have ample reasons for wishing Harold to leave my employ. And as you know, I dislike to refuse a lady's request. However, this employee has been a very valuable one, and to dismiss him, however much I may wish to play the *chevalier*, that is, the gallant knight, is a matter for much thought. I will tell you my decision in exactly one month." He made an elegant bow over Aunt Myriah's hand. "In the meantime, you, my dear Madame Von Wooten, may wish to send for your deed and bank funds.

"And you, Mademoiselle." He lingered longer over his farewell to Marianna, bringing her fingers to his lips and holding her eyes with his. "You must remember that ours is a wicked city, and a few good works should be enough to secure your position with the angels."

Common sense told Marianna she had not been threatened by Jacques Tremaine, that he had meant to compliment her, to describe her willingness to help Christina Dowling as angelic. It was extravagant, of course, but she had been called an angel before. Yet the tone of his voice and the expression in his eyes had not been complimentary. They had been menacing.

Something was going on here she did not understand, but she was sure the hook-nosed man and Cole Taylor were involved in it.

And since I saw the assassination and can identify the killer, I'm involved in it too!

The horror of that knowledge insulated Marianna from her aunt's icy silence riding down in the lift and kept her unconcerned about the thundering scolding she could expect when they reached home.

"I am certain he would have cooperated if you had only asked him," Aunt Myriah would accuse. "You knew I was counting on you. It was your duty to help me after I brought you halfway around the world."

And Marianna would reply the same way, over and over again without really thinking about the words, "I'm sorry, Aunt Myriah. I'm sorry, Aunt Myriah."

Through the glass-paned door of the building, they saw a sea of fog. Its thick, soggy layers blotted out the sky overhead and obscured the city around them. Feeling stranded, Marianna and her aunt looked anxiously for a hack or streetcar, but none was in sight. Then they noticed someone beckoning to them from a carriage that looked ghostly and remote across the avenue.

"I thought you might not be long and if I waited you might take tea with me." It was Christina Dowling—her stylish hat with its sweeping black feathers drooping slightly in the damp air. "After bearding the lion in his den, I feel the need for some refreshment," she continued to explain as she made room for the ladies on the broad leather-upholstered seats and gave her coachman the signal to get underway.

"I know it was foolish of me to ask him for money to help those girls, but it seemed fitting. And when I get a bee in my bonnet, I can't let it alone until it works itself out."

"Why fitting?" Marianna asked, puzzled once again by the beautiful widow's obvious nervousness.

"My dears, he is the owner of most of the slave shops in Chinatown!"

Aunt Myriah's audible sniff voiced her disagreement clearly without the necessity of rudely contradicting her hostess. Marianna also felt skeptical but uncertain.

"I must confess something about that Frenchman terrifies me," Mrs. Dowling leaned forward to confide.

"He gives me the shivers," Marianna replied with an expressive shudder, earning one of her aunt's dark looks.

Remembering the impressive Dowling mansion, Marianna expected to be taken to some fashionable uptown restaurant for tea, but the carriage rolled slowly along the wharves below Telegraph Hill and stopped before a Japanese tea room.

"The English black blends have never appealed to me since I first tried the oriental teas," Christina—she insisted on being called by her first name—explained.

The tea room was built around a tiny garden. On a sunny day the winding paths leading to miniature pagodas and arching bridges were probably charming, but in the fog the scene was dismal. The stunted trees, twisted into intricate shapes, looked grotesque, and the water of the pond, where a few gold and white fish swam slowly, was murky.

Tea was served at low lacquered tables in a room partitioned by screens and dimly lit by candles. Red and yellow paper lanterns glowed overhead but did little to dispel the darkness.

Marianna could see courtesy warring with distaste in her aunt's face, but courtesy won out. Gingerly the old lady lowered herself to a rice mat beside the tea table and took off her gloves.

Their hostess had not missed the expressions and apparently understood their import, for she looked anxiously at Marianna.

"This is delightful," the younger woman responded quickly, careful not to meet her frowning aunt's glance or to squirm uncomfortably on the rice mat. But she could not resist a smile at an enormous orange and black tiger stalking through a bamboo forest and looking ready to pounce, open-mouthed, from the painted screen onto her aunt's towering bonnet.

The tea, however, was delicious. Different from the Chinese jasmine, it tasted tangy with spices and slightly sweet and was served scalding hot in tiny eggshell-thin cups they held around the rims to prevent burning their fingers. A plate of delectable almond cookies, each with a sliver of skinless, blanched almond in the center, accompanied the tea, and even Aunt Myriah unbent enough to eat several.

While they sipped the tea and nibbled on the cookies, their hostess told them about the need for her Chinatown

Girls' Shelter. "The problem is heart-wrenching. Every year hundreds of girls are bought in Canton for $40 apiece and shipped here. The more fortunate ones are put to work in the kitchens or laundries. But others end up in dance halls or houses of ill repute. Few live to be more than twenty, and if they can run away, they have no place to go. Legally they are nothing more than property, and the good people of San Francisco treat them as though they were morally invisible."

Remembering how Cole Taylor said he had bought Mi Ling for her, Marianna squirmed uncomfortably. She did not like the feeling of owning a human being, even if the person benefitted from that ownership.

As a new member of the Ladies' Relief Society, Aunt Myriah must have felt obligated to be concerned, but Marianna noticed how embarrassed her aunt looked each time Christina Dowling mentioned "houses of ill repute" or "slave girls."

"We must do everything we can for these poor unfortunate creatures," her aunt spoke up finally, "but perhaps this is not the right charity for a young girl like Marianna to become involved in."

"I'm not a young girl," she responded promptly and firmly. "I'm a woman, and this is exactly the kind of charity all women should become involved in."

Christina beamed at her and exclaimed as though to herself, "I knew I could count on Cole to pick a woman with some spunk!" Then she proceeded to outline the project for them.

The task ahead was a formidable one. To begin with, they would have to find a place large enough to house thirty or forty girls, and to avoid pressures from landlords, who might also have an interest in thwarting their efforts, they would have to buy rather than rent.

"The house will be my contribution," she assured them, and remembering the cost of real estate in San Francisco, Marianna was impressed. But finding a house was a problem. It should be close to Chinatown to be accessible but, for safety, not actually in it. Then they would have to raise funds to maintain the shelter and recruit a staff, including a nurse or doctor and teachers to train the girls in English and a trade. "I want us to do more than just feed and clothe them. When they leave our shelter, they should be ready to find jobs and support themselves in American society."

Before the last cup was poured from the delicate porcelain pot, Marianna had offered to find the house, and even Aunt Myriah, carried away in spite of herself, had agreed to serve dessert for a fund-raising dinner.

So now I have become a reformer in earnest, Marianna thought as they left the tea garden. She remembered Cole Taylor's prediction and wondered, *Do western men really like eastern ladies who try to change them?* Jacques Tremaine did not. In fact, she would guess the only thing that made him tolerate their efforts was his assurance they would fail.

"I will send someone tomorrow to drive you to look for the house," Christina promised as she left them at the foot of their street. Noting the enthusiasm that set the widow's complexion aglow and made her voice vibrant, Marianna felt at the same time proud to be helping her and envious of her zeal.

She's the real reformer here, Marianna reminded herself. *Wherever she comes from, she fits Cole's idea of the reforming eastern lady to a T.* Unaccountably, that thought caused her spirits, heretofore buoyed up since their meeting with Tremaine, to plunge, and a disheartened Marianna went through the motions of eating dinner and preparing for the midweek prayer service at church.

Harold ate with them, but he said he had no time for the service.

For the first time it occurred to Marianna to ask Harold what exactly he did for his employer. His answer was vague, almost evasive. "I'm in management, involved with handling finances and acquisitions."

"What do you acquire for him?" she prodded, thinking of Christina Dowling's charge that Tremaine owned slaveshops.

"Gold mines mostly, although tonight I'm working on a steamship deal. If we put it through, one of our biggest competitors in supplying the mining camps may be out of business."

Only a few of the faithful were in their pews that night. The minister, looking down the aisles at the scattered upturned faces, made a valiant effort to hide his discouragement. *He misses the Sunday morning glories,* Marianna recalled her father's name for his church members who came only on Sunday mornings. The memory made her feel suddenly homesick.

The pianist had not come, and the organ wheezed too much in the dampness. But they had the Word.

The text for the study was Jonah 1:

> *Now the word of the Lord came unto Jonah the son of Amittai, saying,*
>
> *Arise, go to Nineveh, that great city, and cry against it; for their wickedness is come up before me.*

Jonah in the belly of the whale—Marianna had told the story often to her Sunday school class of preschoolers. Always it had seemed almost like a fairy tale with the fierce whale and the cowardly Jonah as figures of fun. But now on a gloomy night in another wicked city, the familiar words of scripture took on a new meaning.

"Many of us are spiritual Jonahs. We ignore God's call out of fear or out of reluctance to leave the peace and safety of our homes and families. But the call of God is not to be ignored. He prepared a storm and the belly of a whale for Jonah; for us it may be a storm of affliction and a prison of suffering. But we need not wait to be swallowed. We can answer the call when it comes." The young minister's impassioned plea was compelling, and Marianna wondered if his own service in San Francisco was in response to a Jonah's call.

She wondered too if she had been another kind of Jonah, refusing to consider a life in the West with Harold and laughing at her dedicated sister for becoming a missionary nurse and for staying to make her home in the Oregon wilderness. Families and churches, she had told Cole Taylor, were the answers to this city's wickedness, but what chance for change would exist if Christian women and ministers stayed safely in the East while men and scoundrels settled the West?

"Remember, when Jonah finally did his job, not only he but also the entire city of Nineveh was saved."

And God saw their works, that they turned from their evil way; and God repented of the evil, that he had said that he would do unto them; and he did it not.

"The responsibility is awesome, but the rewards of obedience both for us and for those around us are great."

The small congregation was unnaturally silent as they filed from the sanctuary.

"Gloomy young man. His sermons could use some pepping up," Aunt Myriah commented to the neighbors who had shared their carriage with her and her niece.

But Marianna felt, if not exactly inspired, at least enlightened. "Once in a great while, you will hear a sermon or read a scripture meant especially for you," her father had always said. "When that happens, you will know it and know too how to act on it."

For Gloriana the call had been to the mission fields as a nurse. As for herself, Marianna was not sure yet, but she felt she was on the right track with helping Celestials like Mi Ling.

"God knew what he was doing when he brought us to San Francisco," she told her aunt, unconsciously echoing Cole Taylor's words when they had reached their own door.

"I wish you would not speak of God so familiarly, as though he were a next-door neighbor," the old lady retorted, but she had a mist in her eyes and she forgot to give her niece that thundering scolding.

Caught up in the day's events Marianna did not remember the hook-nosed man until she was drifting off to sleep; then her dreams were troubled by mysterious shots that turned into a chain of firecracker explosions and green dragons that kidnapped helpless Chinese girls.

CHAPTER 8

THE FOLLOWING DAY should have dawned fair and sunny. But, although the fog had lifted, a leaden sky drizzled intermittently throughout the morning.

Marianna drooped around the hillside house, ready to be about and doing but feeling trapped by the weather. The glass on the windows steamed and smeared where she pressed repeatedly against it, trying to see through the moisture that beaded and rolled down the panes outside. The dampness had penetrated inside too. The pages of the book Marianna was trying to read felt clammy in her hands, while the fire smoked sluggishly in the fireplace.

In contrast Aunt Myriah was all bustle and energy. "Only two days to prepare for this dinner," she had announced as she walked down the stairs that morning, "and me with no recipes but what I have in my head." Retrieving a prize-winning recipe for chocolate cake from her memory had occupied all her time as well as Mi Ling's since breakfast. With the bewildered maid at her elbow, Aunt Myriah had stirred and tasted and stirred and tasted some more.

"Something's still missing," she would announce every few minutes, sending Mi Ling off in a flutter to find the spice or flavoring or dollop of butter she seemed to remember should be added.

"I have never eaten chocolate cake," the Chinese girl confided in Marianna.

"You'll love it," Marianna assured her, but so far bits of the little test patties that Aunt Myriah periodically popped into the oven had left Mi Ling unimpressed.

"I make Chinese cookies just in case," she whispered with a look of sympathy at Marianna's aunt.

Christina Dowling had said someone would call to take her house hunting for the shelter around two in the afternoon. Although Marianna doubted much hunting could be conducted on such a day, she dressed in a heart-lifting primrose walking dress to counteract the gloomy weather and sat beside the window.

"Looking as pretty as a picture and just as useless," her aunt grumbled on one of her quick trips from the kitchen through the parlor.

At exactly two o'clock a familiar buggy pulled up at the gate. The accordian-shaped top was up, but Marianna recognized the gray horse that immediately put its head over the fence to nibble at the wet flowers. The driver was wearing a corduroy jacket and high boots, like those Marianna had seen on gold miners; however, the usual black hat and the arrogant set of his broad shoulders were enough to identify Cole Taylor even before she could see his face.

That face looked shadowed and grim through the window. After seeing the white envelope in his hand, Marianna felt a little gulp of fear catch at the base of her throat.

Rushing to the door, she flung it open.

"Now that's what I like—a lady eager for my company. Miss me while I was gone?" The grimness had vanished, and he was grinning delightedly.

"I didn't know you were gone," Marianna faltered, then laughed as his expression fell dramatically.

"For your information I have been north to Eureka where I had the good fortune to pick up, among other things, a letter with your name on it." He presented the thick envelope with a flourish as though he were offering a precious jewel. A letter in San Francisco was an event. Steamer Day, when a steamship arrived from Panama with the mail from the East, brought thousands to the docks.

This letter was not from the East; yet Marianna's heart was warmed to see her missionary sister's firm slanted script in pencil, of course, to guard against smears if the mail should "happen to get wet."

"Am I being overly curious if I ask who Miss Marianna Windemere of Philadelphia might know in the wilds of Oregon Territory? I hope it's not another rival for poor Harold."

Marianna ignored the hinted reference to his own supposed rivalry. Resisting the impulse to tear the letter open and read it on the spot, she tucked it carefully away from Cole's openly prying eyes into the depths of her reticule. "You are overly curious, but I don't mind telling you it's from my sister, Gloriana."

"Married sister?" He continued to probe, probably remembering the name "Norton" rather than "Windemere" on the envelope.

"She married one of your wild westerners," Marianna admitted, "and plans to live happily ever after in a place called Applegate Landing."

"I know the place—picturesque little community of log cabins, presided over by an old pioneer, Jesse Applegate."

Aunt Myriah came through the arched doorway that topped the kitchen stairs, a mixing bowl under her arm and a large wooden spoon in her hand. "What are you doing here?" was her ungracious greeting. Her eyes looked pointedly at the black boots muddying her entry way and at the wet hat dripping on the carpet from where Cole held it in his hands, and then shifted suspiciously to Marianna.

"He brought a letter from Gloriana," she explained quickly.

"More than that. Christina sent me to help Marianna with some house hunting."

How he managed to extricate her from the house, directly under the nose, as it were, of her hostile aunt, Marianna would never fully understand. She suspected, though, that it had something to do with an engaging grin in a handsome face and heavy helpings of flattery.

"I think your aunt is beginning to like me or perhaps she feels some competition will warm up that cold-blooded stepson of hers."

"Harold is not cold-blooded," Marianna snapped defensively, then clenched her teeth in frustration. Five minutes alone with Cole Taylor and he had her seeing red already. The man seemed to delight in teasing her. She knew her all-too-predictable reactions egged him on, but she couldn't seem to stop.

The air outside was like a liquid curtain, so heavy with moisture she could almost touch it. Muddy water stood in puddles in the terraced garden and trickled along ruts in the unpaved street.

"Isn't it a bit wet for exploring?" Marianna looked dubiously at the skimpy buggy top and then at the clouds crouching in soggy layers over the city, the soft gray swells just touching the hilltops.

"A native San Franciscan never lets a little rain stop him," Cole responded with an airy wave at the sky. He pulled a shiny oilskin robe from under the seat and tucked it around her legs. "Wait until you've been here through one of our winters—no snow but plenty of fog."

Marianna started to say she had no intention of seeing a San Francisco winter but, recalling the minister's "Jonah" sermon, thought better of it. She was through with ultimatums and pronouncements. Besides, she had the uncomfortable feeling any more I-will-not statements might be taken as I-dare-you impertinence by her Heavenly Father.

"I'm glad at least one Windemere has a fondness for us westerners," Cole said with a sideways glance at her that promised mischief. He had to pull on the reins with both hands and give a sharp shake to distract his horse from the daisy bed it had just finished demolishing.

Marianna took a moment to realize he was referring to

her sister's western marriage. "You really ought to do something about your voracious beast." She skirted the subject. "It isn't normal for a horse to eat like that."

"What does her husband do?"

"Whose husband?"

"The husband of this rebel sister you don't want to talk about."

Marianna sighed with a mixture of exasperation and resignation. She might as well answer his questions. He wouldn't stop until she did anyway. "I gather he has something to do with hauling freight over the mountains and building roads through the forest or something like that. Whatever it is, his work requires him to leave Gloriana alone often in a cabin in the middle of the wilderness."

"Does she mind?"

"Of course she minds! At least I would suppose so. I know I would. In fact, I don't know how she bears it. Myself, I love a city with throngs of people, houses crowded closely together, everyone moving and doing things. I like civilized trees—nice comfy ones that children can climb and hang their swings in—even a small woodlot terrifies me."

Cole chuckled. "You wouldn't like Eureka then," he said and began to tell her about the groves of redwoods that surrounded the town with the imagination-sparking Greek name.

The buggy rolled slowly up and down the streets around Chinatown. The area was filled with storefronts and lodging houses, several of them empty but none with the special homelike quality for which Marianna was looking.

"It doesn't have to be a mansion," she assured him, "but it should have something heart-warming about it, the kind of place that's both comfortable and endearing. I prefer comfort to luxury; it's more homey."

"You talk like a born homemaker."

"I am," she confided with a little smile for her inner visions of overstuffed armchairs by a crackling fire and checked red gingham curtains. "It's my one gift. In our family everyone has always been so talented—the kind of people who accomplish things and make a difference in the world. With Gloriana, it's nursing. Juliana plays the piano and sings like an angel. I discovered early that the one thing I do well is homemaking, and I love it. I promised myself that someday I would have a big house on a tree-lined boulevard and a dozen children." Marianna stopped abruptly and blushed to match her primrose gown.

Cole, however, was intent on his driving and did not seem to notice. They had in fact traveled more than a block up a particularly steep street to stop in front of a large rooming house before he commented abruptly, "I don't think your Harold is up to it."

San Francisco had no truly old buildings. Nonetheless, the rooming house had a history, according to the slatternly landlady who waited to show them through her domain. "Survived the big fire of '51 and the riots in '53." She pointed proudly to flame-licked ceiling beams and a taped window as relics of those events. Individual rooms overflowed with what Marianna took to be dancehall-girl finery. The common parlors looked as though a herd of rough miners had regularly tramped on the floor, leaned against the walls, and drummed booted feet on its furniture.

"The real test is the kitchen," Marianna whispered to Cole. They both shuddered at that dark, unappetizing room, where the odorous memories of a thousand meals still clung to the walls and the stove.

"What is she asking for the place?"

Cole consulted a list in his inside coat pocket. "$60,000."

Marianna sputtered angrily, "It's not worth a tenth of that!"

"Oh, it's worth it all right. A few years ago she could have gotten twice that. In fact, in '49 the government paid $7,000 a month rent for a shack to be used as a customs house, and a tent large enough to hold a bar and a few roulette tables rented for $40,000 a year. Now, though, property values have fallen somewhat." He sounded oddly wistful, as though the passing of those days of wild excesses were something to be regretted.

"Were you here then?" Cole, she realized suddenly, rarely talked about himself; always, this strange, wild mushroom of a city filled his conversation.

For an answer he pulled a heavy gold watch from a vest pocket. When she pushed the little catch that opened the cover, it played something that sounded vaguely like "Oh, Susannah." The inscription read, "San Francisco, California, 1849."

"You were a '49er!"

"You make that sound like a rare disease. The gold in that watch and a few nuggets I've been saving for something special . . ." He glanced pointedly at Marianna's ring finger. ". . . are all I have left of my one and only gold strike. But I'll never forget the excitement of panning on the Sacramento when there was a miner every few yards. That and the I-found-it feeling when you wash away the dirt and find a sparkling nugget at the bottom of the pan will stay with me for the rest of my life."

They went from building to building, rejecting one for its size, another for its depressing surroundings, and as they looked, they talked, almost like old friends.

"Things happen quickly here," Cole told her, and she could well believe it. An acquaintance begun casually on a ship just a few weeks ago was beginning to seem like a lifetime of shared memories.

Marianna soon noticed Cole's little ceremony of helping her from the buggy at each stop. Instead of offering his hand, he would reach for her waist and then wait until her hands were securely on his shoulders before lifting her slowly, his laughing eyes never leaving hers, to the ground.

"Don't do that," she said finally with an annoyed little twist to dislodge the hand still lingering on her waist.

"Don't do what?" he asked innocently. His rounded eyes with their dusky fringe of lashes would have done credit to an angel, Marianna thought irreverently, though she wasn't sure whether they would better suit the heavenly or the fallen variety.

"Don't help me like that. It makes me feel like a . . . like a floozy!"

Marianna thought she heard a suppressed laugh, but thereafter Cole let her scramble out of the buggy on her own. As though in sympathy with his owner, suddenly Cole's horse developed a knack for stopping directly over a puddle or just far enough away from a raging gutter to require an undignified leap if she wanted to keep her skirts and shoes dry.

"I have to hand it to you eastern ladies," Cole said after a while. "You'll go to any length to maintain your distance and your dignity."

Aware her leaps not only looked undignified but were probably exposing an immodest amount of ankle and limb, Marianna responded snappishly, "And you western men will go to any length to make us appear foolish."

"Would I do that to you?" Cole protested. She heard him add under his breath, "Besides, it doesn't take much."

In two hours of looking, the only house they liked was a three-story building with enough towers and balconies to give the owner the feeling of living in a castle.

"It's marvelous," Marianna breathed, falling instantly for the intricate gingerbread decorating the gables and the profusion of little attics and hideaways hinted at by tiny windows tucked away near the roof.

Cole consulted his list and shook his head. "Won't do."

"But the house is perfect! It's close to Chinatown. It has enough room for several dozen girls. What could possibly be wrong with it?"

Cole looked at her with a masked expression that she supposed meant she should take his word for it.

"Cole, I want that house for the shelter. If you don't think it's right for us, you'll have to tell me why."

"Jacques Tremaine owns it."

Momentarily she was taken aback, not so much by his words, but by the anger with which he spoke. Then glancing at Cole from under lowered lashes, she dismissed the objection with an arch laugh. "Oh, if that's all you're worried about, we'll just get Christina to ask him for it. If she says 'pretty please'' he might even give it to her.''

''What?'' His question was both explosive and furious.

Hastily Marianna stammered an explanation of Christina's visit to Tremaine and his $10,000 contribution. ''He seemed so taken with her that I just thought he would give her anything. That's all I meant, really.''

Cole still scowled and his response was curt. ''Taken with her? Of course he's taken with her. He has been since the moment he saw her and that was well before her husband was killed.''

Marianna felt a stab of jealousy. So that was it! Cole Taylor was as serious about Christina Dowling as Harold had said. All his talk about his feelings for her and his ridiculous claim-jumping were no more than meaningless flirtation. *He's just amusing himself while he waits for the widow to come out of mourning.* The realization made her furious with herself as well as with him. How could she have been so gullible?

''I don't think you need worry,'' she said coldly to make it clear she had no interest whatsoever in interfering in his relationship with Christina. ''She seems to loathe him.''

''How do you know that?'' Cole's puzzled look could have meant he was eager to hear her answer or he was surprised by her icy tone.

''She said so.''

By unspoken agreement they looked at no more houses. However, instead of driving her directly home, as Marianna had assumed he would, Cole went to the docks. A battered steamer lay anchored at the pier. Even in the rain, which had begun to fall steadily, she could see that there had been a recent fire on the deck. Some of the timbers at the stern looked cracked and splintered, evidence that the ship had been involved in a near-collision.

''Is that the steamship you sailed on from Eureka?'' Marianna remembered suddenly her impression of a grim shadow over Cole's face when she had first seen him that morning.

Cole nodded. "It was a foggy night, and we had to creep down the coast to keep our bearings. We were just outside the Golden Gate when the trouble started. The first mate noticed a passenger lowering one of the dinghies, but before he could sound the alarm, fire was reported on the forward deck. We left the captain alone on the bridge while we, passengers and crew, went to fight the fire. It wasn't anything serious, just some oily rags that had been piled up and set to burning. The flames licked at the deck but didn't really catch hold—I thank God for that. Without the wet weather, it might have.

"We had the fire out and were looking around again for that passenger when the ship's bell began to ring. The captain had seen a three-master looming out of the fog and was trying to warn it off. The crew hadn't heard it because of the sound of our own engines and the fire's keeping everyone busy.

"But she had seen us, she couldn't help it with that fire acting as a beacon on the deck and, instead of veering off, was coming straight ahead." Cole had told the story to this point unemotionally, as though he were telling her about some common seagoing occurrence. Now he paused and Marianna wondered if he were reliving that nightmare.

"What happened then?" she prompted, hardly aware that she had grabbed his arm.

Cole cleared his throat, removed her hand gently but firmly, and finished in an expressionless voice. "We took a chance on heading the right direction in the fog, poured on the steam, and shot through the Golden Gate.

"But I was standing in the stern as she just grazed us. Marianna, I saw the name of the ship that tried to ram us. It belongs to Jacques Tremaine."

CHAPTER 9

"HE GAVE ME THE SCOLDING OF MY LIFE," Christina Dowling told Marianna. The widow sat in a fan-backed, gilt-edged chair in a sunlit parlor of her Park Place mansion. With the sun on her glorious red hair and her green eyes flashing indignantly she could have been an outraged queen. "I resent being dictated to," she snapped, with more than a trace of resentment in the look she gave her guest.

"I had no idea he wouldn't approve," Marianna explained, "or that he would dare to mention it to you." She had come to report to Mrs. Dowling on the failure of her first house-hunting attempt and had walked in on the tail end of a scene that made her cringe with embarrassment.

"Christina, I won't have you playing games with Jacques Tremaine!" She could still hear Cole Taylor lecturing—no, more like threatening—her hostess. His voice's stand-and-deliver quality would have made Marianna capitulate or at least retreat immediately. But Christina was made of sterner stuff.

"What we ought to do is get out the carriage and go ask Jacques Tremaine for that house. No, don't look so frightened. I only said we ought to do it. We won't. What really infuriates me is that deep down I know that Cole is right. He usually is."

Her green eyes swept Marianna with a speculative gleam. "I'll bet he laid down the law to you, too."

"He was so angry that when we drove down on the docks, I thought he was going to dump me in the water." Marianna joined her hostess's laughter with relief. Whoever had equated red hair with a temper had been right. Every ounce of her emotional energy had been spent in trying to smooth the troubled waters Cole had left when he stormed out. And the disgusted glare he had raked over her on his way out occupied a prominent spot in her mind.

"Don't feel too bad about it," Christina urged her. "Men often react with anger when something has frightened them. Cole was just afraid for you."

"He has no reason to be afraid for me," Marianna started, then faltered, remembering Tremaine's half-threat and the very real menace in the eyes of the hook-nosed man. "The person he's really afraid for is you. He says Tremaine has been 'after you' since before your husband died."

Christina dropped her glance to yesterday's newspapers spread across a table. *The Chronicle, The Bulletin, The Star, The Alta Californian*—all featured the fire on Cole Taylor's steamship and the near-miss outside the Golden Gate. The stories differed, however, in suggesting a cause for the mishaps. *The Chronicle* and the *Alta Californian,* which had printed interviews with members of the crew, claimed the incidents were related and called for city officials to find and punish the pirates. *The Bulletin* and *The Star* spoke of tragic accidents and the need for better safety measures by steamship owners.

"Marianna, I wasn't a Christian when I came to San Francisco in '49." Christina began slowly, not looking at her guest. She took a deep breath and the words tumbled out. "I worked at the El Dorado where Jacques Tremaine was a dealer." They had been friends, more than friends. Then she had met Sam Dowling. He had been decent and lonely, and he had believed in her. "He helped me learn how to fill what he called that 'God-shaped vacuum' in my life." She lifted her eyes to meet Marianna's. "I can't explain to you the change that made. Suddenly anything was possible. We were married; Sam struck gold; I became a respectable San Francisco matron with three adorable babies."

Her voice shook and Christina brushed away a trace of moisture from her eyelashes. "When Sam was killed a year ago, Cole suspected Jacques. I wouldn't believe him, but now I do. Marianna, we have to do something before he kills Cole too!"

But what could they do? Two women alone in the middle of a battle they did not fully understand, against men who would not hesitate to kill them.

"But we're not alone," Marianna said, taking the lead with more confidence than she actually felt. "We are Christians, and we can pray." And with hands joined they sent their appeals heavenward.

Heaven, however, seemed remote in San Francisco during the summer of 1855. "God's in his heaven, and Washington is far away" was the anything-goes slogan of the city's lawless element. With rumors and threats of violence echoing in her head even Marianna could almost believe it. "You don't have to feel God watching to know He is," she reminded herself. Still it would have been comforting to hear a voice or see a flash of lightning—something to show the Lord was on the job.

Why does God let the sun shine so brilliantly on such a wicked city? Marianna wondered later that day as she and Mi Ling rode the streetcar down Sacramento Avenue. The view through the open car windows was breathtaking. The street plunged with dizzying straightness all the way to the docks where the masts of toy-sized ships floated on a china-blue bay. To the north a clipper, its white sails spreading in the stiff sea winds, was spotlighted by a blaze of sun in the Golden Gate. The top-of-the-world scene was heart-lifting and completely out of keeping with Marianna's mood.

She felt emotionally tired. The morning with Christina Dowling had contributed to that feeling, of course; the volatile widow's quick swings from anger to laughter to tears had moved, but also amazed Marianna. Christina was sincere in all her feelings, Marianna had no doubt of that. She was less certain, though, what to make of the tangle of fears and accusations. How much was based on fact and how much on nightmare? Losing her husband to such a violent death could have affected the way she looked at things.

Nonetheless, Marianna's depression hinged on more than her visit with Christina Dowling. Since yesterday she had felt torn apart, wrenched in two different directions by conscience and by loyalties. When she had looked at Cole Taylor's battered and blackened steamship, a picture had flashed across her mind of a foggy evening and Harold sitting at her aunt's dining table while saying he could not attend church with them. "I'm working on a steamship deal," he had said. "If we put it through, one of our biggest competitors in supplying the mining camps may be out of business." She had started to tell Cole, then choked back the words as she realized what they meant.

"Marianna, if you know something, tell me!" Cole had barked at her. "Men's lives are at stake."

Those words had haunted her through a sleepless night and throughout her talk with Christina Dowling. She still was not sure she believed Jacques Tremaine was the villain painted by both Cole and Christina. She was even less ready to believe Harold was involved in piracy. But she was convinced Cole was in danger and the hook-nosed man was somehow involved, and, as Christina had said, Cole was usually right. She had to tell him what she knew.

Why can't I stop being a Jonah? Marianna grumbled to herself. Jonah's reluctance to do the right thing had landed him in the belly of the whale. Her own reluctance to tell the truth had landed her, at best, in an uncomfortable situation. She couldn't ask Cole Taylor to come to her aunt's house; her aunt might turn him from the door or, worse, overhear what her niece had to say. She couldn't commit her information to a letter either. She would have no idea whom to trust with delivering it, and she had a vague idea that if she did not put anything in writing, she would somehow be protecting Harold without betraying her own conscience.

Her only choice was to find Cole and give him the information in person, and since she had heard him tell Christina he was going to his club, Marianna had made up her mind to follow him there.

It was, she knew, a highly improper thing to do. Young Philadelphia-bred ladies did not follow a gentleman to his home, his club, or anywhere else. *This is not Philadelphia. No one will even notice,* Marianna had assured herself repeatedly. However, Mi Ling's stiff posture and unyielding expression as she accompanied Marianna shook that assurance, and several times she was on the point of turning back.

"It is not done," the maid, raised to an even stricter sense of propriety and decorum than Marianna's Philadelphian standards, had protested. "Graceful lady not enter room of man, even of own husband." To Mi Ling the word *graceful* seemed to encompass all ladylike virtues, and Marianna suspected her own insistence on this visit had caused her to fall a long way in the Chinese girl's eyes.

Marianna knew Cole lived at his club and knew too he was part of a volunteer fire brigade. What she did not know was that the two were one and the same. "The '49er Club on Jackson Street," she was told when she asked for directions.

That address was the site of a three-story fire station. Painted white and trimmed with red and gold, the building looked businesslike but still a bit fancier than the municipal fire stations back east. San Franciscans apparently took their volunteer fire fighting seriously.

The huge folding doors at the ground level of the station were open as Marianna and Mi Ling approached. Inside was a large red and black fire engine, gleaming with brass appointments—a brass bell on top to be rung while speeding toward a fire, brass fittings on the hoses, and brass trim that completely circled the engine. The company's name had been painted in gold letters across the side, and the white wheels had been edged with gilt. Since there was no sign of horses, probably the stable was back of the station. But Marianna guessed the team that pulled such a gorgeous engine must be matched white chargers.

Three men dressed in overalls and red kerchiefs were busy washing the already spotless engine.

"Could you tell me where I might find Mr. Cole Taylor?" Marianna's question, spoken in a nervous, reedy voice drew three pairs of eyes in her direction.

One man, older than the rest and with a grizzled gray beard, smiled a kind smile, made garish by his several gold teeth, wiped his hands on a spotless rag—obviously everything to do with this fire station had to be immaculate—and hurried toward her.

"Cole's upstairs, ma'am. I'll just step up and call him."

Feeling three pairs of curious eyes on her, Marianna declined hastily. She could not bear to talk to Cole in front of these men. The bearded man looked inclined to argue, then, perhaps seeing her embarrassment, showed her a narrow stairway winding around a well-greased fire pole. Imagining a stampede of men sliding down it, Marianna prayed fervently that no fire alarm would sound while she and Mi Ling were on the stairs and started bravely upward.

Mi Ling maintained a determined silence. Her eyes had not left the toes of her shoes since they had entered the station, and Marianna winced as she realized the agonies of embarrassment the Chinese girl was suffering for her.

The stairs ended at the second floor, but the fire pole continued to the top story. "Probably the sleeping quarters are above and the public rooms are here," Marianna told Mi Ling, more for the comfort of hearing her own voice than because she thought Mi Ling would feel relieved that they were entering a public room rather than a private sleeping area.

She was not prepared, though, for the shocked silence

that greeted their entry. The room was large and carpeted, with a billiard table at its center and ceiling-high bookshelves covering one wall. Heavy blue drapes framed a row of windows facing the street, and the light from those windows fell on what seemed a crowd of stunned masculine faces.

"May we help you, miss?" One young man, quicker than the others to struggle into his coat, rushed at her. The united sound of his *we* conveyed a sense of male solidarity against this feminine intrusion, and for a panicky moment Marianna considered dashing back through the door and sliding out of sight down the fire pole.

"I would like to see Mr. Cole Taylor," she answered finally in what she hoped was a businesslike tone, even if her voice trembled slightly.

Chairs were quickly brought for her and Mi Ling, and the women sat down almost cautiously on the edges. Trying to appear unconcerned, Marianna glanced casually around her. She noted a large temperance banner above a cavernous fireplace and a line of symbolically overturned mugs on the mantel. Apparently this was one of the fire companies she had read about who had taken the pledge so as not to endanger the safety of the city by being intoxicated during a fire. Huge paintings hung on the walls, most of them of sailing ships or seascapes with a few scenes that looked like gold diggings and mining camps. The room smelled of strong coffee and cigars, and though the men avoided looking in her direction, the atmosphere fairly crackled with outrage at her invasion of their privacy.

"I always thought a men's club would be filled with indecent pictures and have beer mugs sitting on the floor," Marianna whispered to an unresponsive Mi Ling. The real thing was less shocking but definitely more comfortable.

A huge wall clock with an enormous swinging pendulum ticked loudly in the hushed room. Watching its creeping hands, Marianna marked one minute, then two minutes gone; the minute hand had started to jump forward a third time when she heard running steps, as though someone were charging downstairs. A second later Cole Taylor burst through the swinging doors at the back of the room. He had forgotten his coat, and his vest was unbuttoned. His frilled shirt was open at the neck and the sleeves were rolled up, as though he had been elbow-deep in some task she had interrupted.

While she waited, Marianna had prepared a little speech. "I know I shouldn't be here," she was going to say. "I had no choice. It's a matter of life and death." One look at his furious face—the dark eyes flashed, the tan skin flushed a deep red—and she forgot every word.

"I need to talk to you," was all she could think to say.

"Not here!" His voice was curt. His hand grasped her arm so hard it hurt. "In my office." Then he propelled, rather than led, her from the room with Mi Ling almost running on her short, tripping steps to keep up. From behind the still swinging doors, Marianna heard an explosion of bottled-up laughter and thought resentfully, *Just catch me worrying again if it's their lives that are in danger.*

Cole's office was toward the back of the second floor, at the end of a long, ill-lit hallway. Mi Ling refused to go in but accepted a chair placed outside the door. Her lowered head reproached Marianna without any need for words.

The room looked lived in, with papers and books stacked on every available flat surface and two walls of bookshelves so stuffed that volumes were laid atop the upright rows or doubled up two rows to the shelf. A third wall was covered with maps, one of the United States, another of the famous around-the-Horn sea route to San Francisco, and a large one of California set with big gold *X* 's to mark gold strikes. The outside wall held two multipaned windows, uncurtained but topped with bamboo blinds that could be raised or lowered. The windows looked out over busy stableyards and across the rooftops to the crowded shipping docks.

With a quick sweep of his arm, Cole tumbled books and papers from a chair and thrust her into it before he retreated behind a similarly encumbered desk. The clutter nearly obscured the desktop but not enough to disguise its worn, scratched state. Marianna found herself contrasting this hectic, much-used room with Jacques Tremaine's luxurious business setting and laughed.

"I'm glad you find this situation amusing, Marianna. I don't."

Marianna brought her eyes back to Cole's, faltered at the suppressed fury of his expression, and began rather lamely, "I'm sorry. I was thinking of something else."

"What possessed you to come here?"

She took a deep breath. He obviously was not going to make this any easier for her. Might as well plunge in and get it over with. So, pulling off her gloves, she started with the day in Chinatown when the hooked-nosed man had shot into the crowd. She explained about seeing the same man in Tremaine's office, about Tremaine's veiled threat, and finally about Harold's reference on that foggy evening—had it only been two nights ago?—to a steamship deal and to putting a competitor out of business.

"I'm sorry I didn't tell you before," she finished with a little sob in her throat. "I just couldn't bring myself to admit Harold was involved."

She did not know when, during her recital, Cole had moved around to her side of the desk or when he had taken her hands comfortingly in his. Now he was using a handkerchief to dab the corners of her eyes; the giant square of linen felt rough on her skin but was immaculately clean; it smelled faintly of pine-scented soap and salty sea breezes.

"Are the tears because you are frightened for me or because you don't like to get Harold in trouble?"

"Both." Her blue eyes pleaded for understanding. "I don't want anything to happen to you, but I grew up with Harold."

Cole traced a line with his finger along her cheek, then gently outlined her lips.

"You know, Marianna, you're going to have to make a decision soon. Do you want Harold or do you want me?"

His look was gentle, but he had a compelling light in his eyes that she could not meet for long. She felt his breath on her upturned mouth for half a second, then his lips just brushed her cheek. "If I had a brain in my head, I would take you to City Hall right now and force you to marry me," he said huskily, more to himself than to her. "But I'm just crazy enough to want you to come to me on your own."

Marianna tried to speak, couldn't, then tried again and found her voice. "What about Christina Dowling?"

Cole looked startled and Marianna saw his little mocking smile turn up the corner of his mouth. "What about Harold Von Wooten?" he challenged.

The questions hung in the air between them for what seemed minutes but must have been no longer than a few seconds.

"You do know what you're choosing, don't you, Marianna?" The teasing look was gone now. His mouth was almost grim, as though he knew what he was going to say might cost him what he wanted most in the world, but he was determined to say it anyway. "If you choose Harold, you'll go back home to Philadelphia eventually. He's in over his head already with Tremaine, and he won't last long out here. You might even hurry him along if you try hard enough. But if you marry me, it means living in San Francisco, helping make this a decent city; it means trusting me and even staying home with our twelve kids when I travel into gold country."

That last was said with just enough arrogance—the dominant male triumphing over the submissive female—to wipe the tears from Marianna's eyes and set angry sparks to leaping there instead. He apparently had remembered her comment about her sister's life and was trying to impose the same pattern of behavior on her.

Leaping to her feet, she yanked her hands away. With as much dignity as she could muster, Marianna marched toward the door, stopping only on the other side. "It's highly improper of you to propose to me when I am already engaged. But get this straight, Cole Taylor. In the highly unlikely event of a marriage between you and me, you would not be going anywhere without me, no matter how many children we had!" And she slammed the door with a force that reverberated through the fire station and intensified the curious looks that followed her hasty exit.

"The boss has woman trouble," she heard one of the men, still busy cleaning the fire engine, tell his companions.

"I wouldn't mind having that bit of trouble myself."

As long as she lived Marianna would never forget the for-men-only atmosphere of that club and the walls of laughter that had shut her out as surely as if she had not swept past the guards and invaded their territory. "I won't forget it, and I won't forgive it either," she added stormily, though it was questionable whether any of the men involved might care one way or the other.

The experience at the club underscored what bothered her about Cole Taylor. He was so completely male. She wondered if she could ever be truly comfortable with him. Imagine a woman's issuing such ultimatums—choose me or else, live here, work there! Marianna stopped abruptly, causing Mi Ling, who had been behind her on the crowded boardwalk, to trip on her billowing hooped skirt.

Weren't those exactly the kind of ultimatums she had given Harold? No wonder he resented it! "You're getting to sound just like your Aunt Myriah," he had told her more than once.

"Good heavens! I am." For a second she imagined herself twenty years from now, married to Harold, an Aunt Marianna Von Wooten trying to arrange the lives of numerous children or, if she had none of her own, numerous nieces and nephews. The picture made her giggle and caused an anxious Mi Ling to pull her sleeve and point silently to the curious, then knowing looks of passersby.

"It's all right. They just think I've been drinking." The horrified look on the Chinese girl's face convinced Marianna that whatever shreds of dignity and grace had been left to her after the fire station episode were now gone.

With grim determination on her face, the maid took over. She shepherded Marianna past a square, where she showed a tendency to linger and think, along the boardwalk, and into a streetcar.

CHAPTER 10

COLE TAYLOR WAS NOT A COMFORTABLE MAN. He laughed at her, bullied her, rearranged her life to suit himself. So why hadn't she told him straight out she would not marry him?

That question occupied Marianna's every waking thought. While her body went through the motions of helping her aunt prepare for the benefit dinner, her brain was trying to find the answer.

On the one hand was Harold. She had become engaged to him because he fell neatly into the mold she had imagined: he was young and handsome; they knew the same people, believed in the same things, and wanted the same things. But how much of that was true? Did Harold fit the mold or had she fitted him to it, expecting and even demanding changes when something did not suit her?

On the other hand was Cole Taylor. He fit no pattern she had ever imagined; in fact, in some ways he epitomized everything she most wanted to avoid in a husband. He lived in a glamorous but frightening city, which at times seemed to Marianna to be located at the end of the world. He had no family she knew of, and he appeared to be committed to the kind of grandiose pioneer dreams she had most wanted to avoid. But what about his beliefs? She knew how he felt about slavery and the vice and corruption in his city. She knew he attended church, and he had at least mentioned prayer and thanking God.

"Is he sincere in his beliefs?" Unconsciously, Marianna spoke aloud, drawing a disgusted glare from her aunt who was putting the finishing touches on a fourth chocolate layer cake.

"Since I have no idea who *he* might be, I can't answer," the old lady barked testily, then began yelling for Mi Ling to forget her cookies and come help with setting the table. "Marianna is too busy daydreaming to be of any help."

To everyone's amazement, Aunt Myriah's most of all, the Von Wooten stage of the benefit dinner was a huge success. The diners had been scheduled to come in three different shifts with twenty-four to a shift.

They began to arrive a little after six, and even in her abstracted state Marianna could tell something was wrong.

"The soup was cold."

"I don't like my chick'n mashed up 'n' smeared with tomatoes and sticky stuff."

"Nothin' to it but little dabs of this and that."

"Ain't worth no $10 a plate, and I'm gonna tell 'em so."

The grumbles of the guests, most of them men, reached Marianna as they came up the steps. "I gather Mrs. Newcomb's vichyssoise and Mrs. Forela's chicken cacciatore did not go over well," Marianna whispered to her aunt.

For an instant panic showed in Aunt Myriah's eyes; then she squared her shoulders and scrapped her plans for thin slices of cake nestled next to tiny scoops of homemade chocolate and vanilla ice cream. "We were a bunch of silly women to forget we would be feeding hungry men rather than a ladies' sewing circle. Hold them off, Marianna."

With that enigmatic command, Aunt Myriah descended to the kitchen and began shouting orders to Mi Ling.

Fortunately, the diners were not adverse to being entertained while they waited for the next course. Wishing for her sister Juliana's talent, Marianna sat down at the piano and, smiling appealingly, began to sing in a husky contralto.

She started with "Oh, Susannah" and went on to "Swanee River," "Home Sweet Home," and "Amazing Grace." By the time she had reached the end of her admittedly small repertoire and was back to "Oh, Susannah" again, Mi Ling was putting heaped up plates of green salad, thick with large chuncks of tomato and cucumber and garnished with homemade mayonnaise, on the table. From below came the smells of pan-fried chicken and potatoes with onions.

After the guests had eaten the last bites of huge slabs of chocolate cake, their grumbles had turned to smiles, but Marianna was scared witless. From the size of those slices of cake and mounds of ice cream, her aunt must have used up everything she had made, and the second group was coming up the walk.

Peeking out the window, Marianna saw Cole Taylor in the lead, and he looked worried.

"They're starved," he whispered as he came through the door.

"I know, and I think we're out of food. Go see."

He disappeared down the kitchen stairs and did not come back. With no food in sight, Marianna went through her singing act again. This time, though, her voice was hoarse, and she had to ask the guests to sing along. They had gone through "Oh, Susannah" and "Yankee Doodle" three times before Cole appeared, wearing one of Aunt Myriah's wraparound aprons and carrying a large tray.

This time they were served bowls of egg flower soup, delicately laced with egg and flavored with chicken; tiny barbecued chicken wings; and crisply fried won tons. Sweet and sour pork, brown rice fried with egg and bits of fresh onion, and butterfly shrimp followed, with heaping mounds of Mi Ling's cookies for dessert.

Finally, the last group was coming through the front gate.

What now? Marianna asked, doubting if she had the energy to sing another note. Fortunately, the food was somehow, amazingly ready—smoked salmon dressing over crisp lettuce, clam chowder with large chunks of potato and little chunks of onion, poached salmon filets, cracked crab with melted butter, and generous slices of apple pie.

"How did you do it?" Marianna questioned Cole as the last diner walked grinning with satisfaction from the house. "That last dinner I mean. I could see Aunt Myriah's able hand in the first dinner and Mi Ling's in the second, but I know we didn't have any salmon and certainly not any crab in the house."

Cole looked self-conscious but pleased with himself. "It was simple. While that second group was gobbling, I sent Mi Ling running down to the club with a note. We just sort of commandeered the club's evening meal."

"But what did they eat?"

"I suggested they all come here for leftovers and promised we wouldn't charge them more than $10 apiece."

Not all the '49ers, but enough to clean up the last spoonful of chowder, the last broken won ton, and the last fried chicken leg, made an appearance. By midnight over a thousand dollars had been earned for the shelter, and the workers had acquired an assortment of aches and pains, mostly concentrated in their feet.

"I have to say this for your Aunt Myriah," Cole told Marianna, "she rose to the occasion like a thoroughbred."

An impatient, perhaps embarrassed, snort sounded behind him, and Aunt Myriah, followed closely by Mi Ling carrying a hot water bottle, a steaming teakettle, a pan, and a jar of Epsom salts, prodded Cole out of the way. "You can save your flattery, young man. But you were Johnny-On-The-Spot when we needed you, and that's more than I can say for another young scapegrace."

"I told you she was beginning to like me," Cole said loudly enough for the old lady to hear as she hobbled to her room and a well-earned soak.

"Marianna?" The gruff voice carried clearly from the second floor.

"Yes, Aunt Myriah."

"About that question you were asking earlier today. I think my brother would say something like, 'By their fruits ye shall know them.'"

Cole raised a questioning eyebrow.

"It means you're right," Marianna said, laughing. "She is beginning to like you—or at least she approves of your 'fruits.'"

In the parlor the grandfather clock chimed twelve times. The melodious sound echoed through the house, emphasizing the lateness of the hour and urging those still awake to prepare for bed. Marianna took up Cole's hat and coat and went expectantly to the door. However, to her dismay, he slipped neatly past her to the parlor and sprawled comfortably in an overstuffed armchair.

"Where was *your* Harold this evening?"

"Perhaps he had another steamship deal to work on," Marianna countered maliciously and immediately wished she had not; Harold's possible involvement in piracy was nothing to joke about. "Where was *your* Christina?" She gave the word exactly the same twist he had given it. "We could have used her help."

"I'm afraid Christina is wonderful at thinking up projects but not too much help in seeing them through."

"You don't mean she will give up on the shelter idea, do you?" The possibility made Marianna's heart sink. The future of so many girls depended upon the shelter's success.

"Oh, no, she'll stay involved and keep giving money. But it will be up to the rest of us to make the thing work."

Marianna couldn't resist a little smile at the way he said *us*. Apparently he counted himself one of the worker bees rather than part of the queen bee's entourage of drones.

"Speaking of work, hadn't you better start home so you'll be ready for work tomorrow?"

Cole rested his dark head against the crocheted tidy

that protected the back of the chair and closed his eyes. "Can't go back to the club. I stole their dinner. They'll be waiting for me."

"Well, you can't stay here," Marianna told him, her voice raising slightly as she began to feel exasperated.

"Why not? Your aunt's upstairs to protect you, and there's plenty of room here. In fact, there's room enough for the two of us." He shifted over slightly in his chair to offer her a cozy niche in the crook of his arm.

Marianna shook her head and moved behind a broad-backed chair as an extra margin of safety. "Cole, go home."

He shook his head stubbornly. "Not until you quit barricading yourself behind that chair and sit down and talk nicely." His eyes were half closed so that Marianna could not read their expression, but the lazy grin on his face together with the powerfully muscular legs and arms draped over her furniture made him look anything but harmless. As though he could read her mind, Cole beckoned with one hand. "Come on. I'm not dangerous at all . . . at least not while you're wearing that ring."

Her ring! Marianna had taken it off to help in the kitchen; a pearl would melt in a minute in a hot oven. Had she remembered to put it back on? She glanced cautiously at her left hand—no pearl—then unobtrusively slipped the hand in her left pocket. Maybe he wouldn't notice.

"I've always thought the best part of a party was talking about it later," Cole was complaining, "but I see you don't want to play."

She offered his coat and hat with one hand.

"I don't suppose you could hold the coat for me."

"No, I couldn't."

"Then how about seeing me to the door?"

She led the way, uncomfortably aware he stalked behind her. When she turned at the door, he was so close she had to tilt her chin to meet his gaze. "I want you to know how much we appreciate your help tonight," she said, taking a quick step backward, then scolded herself silently for acting like a shy schoolgirl. *No need to let him know how he affects you,* she told herself, trying to appear unaware of the knowing smile on the big man's face. *After all, you have nothing to worry about. He hasn't noticed the missing ring, and he promised.*

Cole laughed, and Marianna had again the uncomfortable feeling he could read her mind.

"You would never make a good poker player, my love." He confirmed that suspicion in a soft voice. Whatever reply she might have made was cut off by a swift kiss. "You see, I did notice."

The door closed quietly, and he was whistling down the steps before she had recovered enough to open her eyes.

"Gloriana said western men are more real. Is that what she meant?" She shook her head to clear it, half disgusted with herself and half pleased.

Then she remembered Gloriana's letter.

Her skirts gathered in one hand, Marianna ran up the stairs with an exuberance that showed no sign of the exhaustion she had been feeling just moments before.

A pale crescent moon cast a faint light through the open window in her room. The light found her engagement ring where she had left it on the dresser. The single giant pearl glowed softly. Marianna picked it up to put it back on, then put it down again.

What if she never put that ring on again? What if she gave it back to Harold, or perhaps Aunt Myriah? Could she live with what that action would mean?

Aunt Myriah would be furious. Harold might be unbearably hurt, though she wasn't too sure about that. Most important, she would be committing herself to life in the West and to marrying one of the wild westerners she had been determined to ignore.

"I'm not sure Mama and Papa would understand," she told herself, looking dreamily toward the star-flecked sky, "but Gloriana would."

It took her a few minutes first to trim and light the lamp on her desk and then to find her sister's letter, crumpled in the bottom of her reticule where she had put it two days before. The familiar handwriting—firm, rounded letters, each exactly the same height—made Marianna long suddenly for her pink-and-lace bedroom back home and for her two sisters, dressed in frilled nightgowns and robes, to join her for midnight "girl talk."

Applegate Landing
July 15, 1855

Dear Marianna,

I have only a few minutes before the freight wagons leave and no time to say this properly. My dear, I am afraid you may be in danger.

Two years ago a fake cavalry company terrorized the settlers here. They killed miners caught alone at their claims, attacked freight wagons, and even wiped out entire settlements. The leader of these cutthroats was a man who called himself John Tilton. (We don't know his real name.) Most of his men were caught, but he escaped, and we have reason to believe he headed for San Francisco.

And now the hard part. The man we knew as John Tilton would be about thirty now. He has brown hair and eyes and a sprinkling of silver at the temples. His manner is charming, with a heavy dose of you-are-the-only-girl-for-me. But he is a brutal killer, capable of any treachery.

I am telling you this, my dear sister, because something about one of the men you described in your letter reminded me of John Tilton. He would be about the same in age and appearance as your Cole Taylor; moreover, I would expect him to be a prominent community figure. The gold and other valuables he and his men stole have never been found. I have often wondered whether he sent them regularly to someone in San Francisco. I remember he received several letters from a place called the El Dorado while he was at Uncle Ralph's medical mission.

Marianna, please stop, look, and listen. I could sense from your letter that you are half in love already. Don't jump into anything until you can discover for certain where John Tilton is. He has no reason to love a Windemere. It was I who exposed him and then caused the battle where he was defeated. If he finds out you are my sister, he will be afraid of what you might know about him, and he will want revenge.

I would suggest you come here, but a wilderness trip has too many opportunities for trouble. You are safer in a big city, surrounded by people.

Be careful, and don't trust anyone.

Your loving sister,
Gloriana

Marianna's hands were trembling, and the face that looked back at her from the mirror was the same ghostly shade as the new moon.

"Dear God, what am I going to do?"

Without thinking she picked up the pearl engagement ring and slipped it back on her finger.

CHAPTER 11

"MARIANNA, I DON'T LIKE THE WAY YOU ARE ACTING. You have been moping around this house for days, as though you were afraid to stick your nose out the door."

Marianna jumped guiltily, then looked with a blank expression, first at the mass of red yarn in her lap and then at her aunt.

"You were winding that for me," was the dry reminder, "though it looks now as though you'll have to untangle it first." Myriah Von Wooten sent a shrewd glance over the top of her sewing glasses, but her fingers did not pause in their knitting.

Knit one, purl two; knit one, purl two. Marianna's eyes followed her aunt's flying fingers. A huge ruby, set in a circle of diamonds, winked in the sunlight streaming through the parlor window. The needles clicked steadily, setting up a counter rhythm to the slow ticking of the parlor clock.

"Mooning over that young man?"

A wary look crept into Marianna's expression, and she began winding her aunt's yarn. "I haven't seen Harold in days."

"I know you haven't. I was talking about your other young man."

There was a hint of accusation in the words, and Marianna felt her face go crimson.

"I have eyes. I know my boy hasn't been paying much attention to you. Acting more like a cousin than a beau, isn't he?"

That was true. After a few passionate kisses her first week in San Francisco and a brief flare-up of jealousy over Cole Taylor, Harold had treated her in an offhand manner that reminded her of her own brothers' casual affection. A peck on the cheek, a companionable hug, some occasional handholding. For the most part his prerogatives as a fiancé had been exercised primarily in telling her what not to do and reminding her she wore his ring.

I don't even think of it as his ring any more. I think of it as the ring that matches Aunt Myriah's pearls. Not to mention as a barrier between her and Cole Taylor. She had seen Cole only once since the night of the benefit dinner. He had taken one look at the pearl on her finger and left without speaking to her.

Marianna sighed. What was she going to do?

The knitting needles stopped. "That sigh was the last straw," Aunt Myriah barked. "Now I want you up and out of this house into the fresh air. You promised that Dowling woman you would find a place for her Girls' Shelter. Well, get dressed and go find it and take that Chinese maid with you. Can't have you running around San Francisco alone in your state. Likely as not you would walk off the edge of a wharf."

More to boost her own spirits than because she expected to meet anyone, Marianna put on her favorite walking dress. The material was a sheer sky-blue wool with white eyelet inserts at the yoked neck and puffed sleeves. A white chip bonnet with an enormous blue satin rose sat atop glossy curls and tied under her chin with narrow blue and white ribbons. After a moment's thought, Marianna added a crocheted half-cape. Its huge mother-of-pearl buttons and graceful border of knotted fringe made her feel elegant enough even for fashionwise San Francisco, and in spite of her initial reluctance,

Marianna found herself looking forward to doing something—anything to shake off the depressed lethargy she had let herself fall into.

Christian had to struggle to get out of the Slough of Despond, Marianna remembered from *Pilgrim's Progress. He had to face his problems head-on, too, straight through the narrow gate and straight up the mountain.* For days she had been asking God to remove her mountain, to clear Cole Taylor, expose the real John Tilton, and free her of the weights of fear and suspicion she had been carrying ever since she had read Gloriana's letter. *Maybe this is one of those mountains I'm supposed to climb.*

She had need of both her cape and her bonnet strings in the crisp coastal winds that puffed and howled through the streets of San Francisco. The gusts caught pedestrians at every corner, whipping Marianna's skirts and setting her hoop dancing around her ankles.

"That wind feels strong enough to blow us to China." She laughed when she could catch her breath.

"Wrong way to go China," Mi Ling giggled in response. "Go Philadelphia instead." Her sleek hairstyle and pajama-style outfit did not take quite the beating from the wind that Marianna's did. Still, she had to hold onto her wide straw hat with both hands, her eyes watered, and her nose as well as cheeks glowed rosily.

Mi Ling had changed dramatically in the weeks since Marianna had met her. Gone was the timid hotel maid, begging pardon for every mistake, real or imagined. In her place was a vividly alive young woman, as gracious and kind as she was pretty. Part of the transformation could be credited, of course, to her escape from the hotel as well as from the fear of what might happen to her if she lost her job and could not pay her family's creditors. Christina Dowling had explained to Marianna what the slave houses were like—"a death sentence for an attractive, sensitive young girl," she had said. The relief that Mi Ling no longer faced such a threat almost made up for Marianna's discomfort over those indentured-servant papers.

"Don't sign those papers over to Mi Ling until she's married or goes back to China." Cole had anticipated Marianna's reaction. "Since she's not a citizen, she has no protection other than her obligation to you."

Mi Ling appeared to find that obligation neither unusual nor intolerable. Continually she found ways to say thank you—an exquisite arrangement of dried grasses on Marianna's dresser; a tiny box, covered with rose-colored silk and embroidered with gold and white butterflies, in which to keep her cameo; a delicate handmade screen with designs woven of dried wheat stalks to shield her from the heat of the fireplace.

Yet the biggest part of Mi Ling's change had been internal rather than external, for Mi Ling was now a Christian. Uncomfortable as she was about her legal hold over the maid, Marianna had more or less decided not to mention religion to her. *She can remain free spiritually at least,* Marianna had rationalized. She had not stopped to consider the consequences of that kind of freedom or the eternal price Mi Ling might have paid for Marianna to soothe her own smarting conscience.

Ultimately Mi Ling had asked about Christ on her own. "I see you angry, you take this book you call Bible and then everything peaceful," she had said. "Please explain me why." When the story of redemption had been told, the girl had accepted with an eagerness that showed clearly her spiritual hunger. Her wistful "Why I not told before? Waste much time!" would stay with Marianna for the rest of her life. Never again would she forget the right of every human being to hear about the Lord and every Christian's obligation to tell about Him. "How then shall they call on him in whom they have not believed? and how shall they believe in him of whom they have not heard? and how shall they hear without a preacher?"

Not only have I become interested in one of Gloriana's wild western men, but I'm also catching the missionary spirit. Marianna could not help laughing at herself. She tried to remember what else she had vowed not to become involved with.

Walking the streets of San Francisco on a windy day was more than difficult. With no curves to break its progress, the wind swept between the straight rows of buildings, gathering force as it went. When they tried to walk up a hill, the wind was in their faces, pushing them back down. When they tried to walk down, the wind was behind, pushing so that they had to run in place to keep from being flung headlong down the hill.

With the wind bullying them and easier downhill slopes tempting, they eventually found themselves in the market area along the old harbor.

"Water come to here when we arrive from China," Mi Ling explained. "Then they fill in with sand to make more room. City grow 'round ships."

In fact, the market still resembled a harbor with sand instead of water drifting around the piers and a row of stranded ships ranged along a weather-beaten wharf as though waiting to load or unload cargo. Looking at those ships, Marianna could almost imagine the frenzied excitement of '49 when gold was found on the American River—the hundreds of ships sailing into the bay, the excited crewmen jumping ship to join the prospectors in the goldfields, the abandoned vessels—often with their cargoes unloaded—left to rot in the water.

"The city should preserve this market as living history!" Marianna surprised herself not only with her enthusiasm but also with her appreciation for San Francisco's brief, spectacular past. *I'm beginning to sound like Cole Taylor. And I swore I would never catch the western fever!*

Most of the ships were in use. An old three-master was a store ship. Customers climbed a gangplank to reach the deck, then entered the hold down a flight of narrow steps where rope the size of a man's wrist provided a prickly railing. A small sloop had become a barber shop. A big sign hanging from the yardarm advertised hot baths and scented steaming towels. One large hull had actually had a small hotel built inside it. A four-sided, three-storied building with regular rows of square windows rose where the masts had been.

In a ship with an unpretentious sign that simply identified without naming Chowder House, diners sat at plank tables on keg chairs in a deck cabin so small that elbows at one table prodded backs at the next. Little remodeling had been done. Except for its missing sails, the ship looked ready to weigh anchor and put to sea. Ropes looped about the masts. The windows in the cabins were portholes. And the food was prepared in the ship's galley and brought to the diners in heavy earthenware dishes, calculated to remain upright and in place in spite of the rolling deck of a sailing ship.

Marianna looked around her. She was beginning to sense the germ of an idea. Most of the help in the chowder house were Oriental, which meant that in spite of the Cape Cod atmosphere, Chinatown must be close by. The quarters were small but immaculately clean, and Marianna remembered from her own experience on shipboard that sailing vessels could house a large number of people with amazing comfort and efficiency.

"It's perfect!" she told Mi Ling excitedly. "Living quarters, a galley already made, and the hold can be adapted for classrooms."

"Not many entrance. Easy to protect." Mi Ling nodded.

"Protect? Why would we need protection?" The idea startled Marianna. She had envisioned a thriving home and school, almost a community center like the settlement houses that were beginning to spring up in poor neighborhoods back East. Not a fortified island in the midst of hostile neighbors.

Mi Ling tried to explain. "You help Chinese girls but men make much money from girls, not want to lose profit."

It had occurred to Marianna they might face some opposition, but she had thought in terms of legal action, petitions, a battle to get public opinion on their side. She had even tried to face the possibility that they would have to protect some of the girls, as Cole had protected Mi Ling, by making them indentured servants or apprentices.

She had not considered violence. Probably Mi Ling was right. In a community where murderers were hanged by vigilantes rather than by the authorities, where gangs of thugs roamed the streets looking for a drunken miner with a bag of gold or a careless citizen with a full purse, where an assassin could murder a spectator at a parade and no one even notice. Of course, in such a place a simple, humane undertaking like opening a girls' shelter could result in violence.

Careful, Marianna. You're beginning to develop a passion for this city. If you're not careful, you'll become an ax-wielding reformer ready to storm the bars and chop up the roulette wheels.

Several abandoned ships were not being used. One, the stripped remains of what had once been a stately clipper, tugged at Marianna's heartstrings. It looked so forlorn, stranded and deserted on the beach. What had happened to the crew? Why hadn't they returned? Surely, they couldn't all have found gold. Somewhere she had heard that only one in fifty had taken as much as $2,000 out of a claim. Probably they had gone from one gold field to another, always expecting to be the ones to shout "Eureka!" at the next strike. From what she had seen, gold fever appeared to be an incurable disease.

Amazingly, the clipper had no owner.

"She was abandoned, ma'am," explained a man whose leathery bronze skin, ragged middy blouse, and corduroy trousers held in place by wide suspenders exactly fit Marianna's mental image of a seaman-turned-prospector. "That means that she belongs to anyone who claims her as salvage."

Marianna could barely contain her excitement until they reached home. Not stopping to answer her aunt's questions, she flung a brief "We found it!" over her shoulder and dashed upstairs to pen a quick note to Christina Dowling. Then, with a vague feeling that salvage must be claimed by taking physical possession of the ship, she dispatched Mi Ling to deliver the note and headed back to literally sit on her find.

Caught up in her plans, Marianna did not notice a sleek

carriage pull up behind her or an elegant gentleman with an ebony cane descend and follow her along the boardwalk.

"You are in a hurry, mademoiselle. Are you, *peut-être,* busy about your good works? Or could it be another visit on business, no doubt, to that absurd teetotaling '49er Club?" The sneering voice with its hint of menace nearly stopped Marianna's heart, but she somehow kept walking.

"I am surprised to see you on foot, Monsieur Tremaine. Taking a constitutional or perhaps stalking some unsuspecting Chinese girl?" Her breath caught in her throat even as she uttered that bit of impertinence. It was useless to tell herself not to provoke him. The man made her skin crawl, much as a slithering snake or a huge black widow spider would.

He caught up with her and shortened his stride to match her own. "That was, of course, a joke, *n'est-ce pas?* " He smiled politely, but his eyes reminded her of ice—slick and treacherous. "You American ladies have such a delightful sense of humor. A Frenchman can only be charmed.

"And for how much longer can our city expect to enjoy the presence of such a charming and witty young lady? Your friends and family in Philadelphia must be desolate at your long absence."

Marianna disciplined her tone to be impersonal, though she longed to match sneer with sneer. "Not so nearly desolate as my sister will be if I leave San Francisco before I see her."

"I was under the impression you would be leaving as soon as I found it convenient for your long-suffering fiancé to leave my employ."

"But that was before I heard from my sister. Now I must wait for her to visit." She was making up her story as she went along.

"This sister you mention, do you correspond often with her?"

"All the time. We must have letters coming and going on every ship. One of her letters was even on that steamship that was nearly sunk. A mishap involving one of your ships also, wasn't it?" She glanced at him, hoping to see some reaction to her bombshell. Tremaine's face was emotionless, except for what might have been a slight tenseness around his mouth.

"You are fortunate to have a sister so close as Oregon Territory. Myself I have a sister also, but she is far away in Paris. I have not seen her since I left home two years ago. But, my dear Miss Windemere, as much as I enjoy walking with you, I have my carriage. Could I take you wherever it is you are going so rapidly?"

Remembering suddenly Mi Ling's warning about danger to the shelter and remembering too that Tremaine was one of those men who profited from misery, Marianna stopped abruptly. She didn't dare let him know about the ship; he would probably find a way to keep them from claiming it as salvage. At the same time the glint in his eye told her she had better not get in his carriage.

"I've enjoyed our little chat," she told him with such a pleasant smile that his eyebrows went up a fraction of an inch in surprise, "but I must decline the ride. I have some, uh, shopping to attend to." She glanced sideways quickly, saw only a tobacco shop, and mentally gave herself a swift kick. Prevaricating was not a skill for which her upbringing as a minister's daughter had prepared her.

Tremaine looked briefly at the shop and then seized her hand. "Of course, a gift for your pipe-smoking uncle and brother-in-law." His lips were moist on her wrist, and she willed herself not to shudder. "Since you will not ride with me, will you be so kind as to deliver a message to your dear aunt? Please tell Madame Von Wooten that I find my need for her stepson is not nearly so pressing as hers, and yours too *certainment*. I will inform Harold tomorrow I no longer require his services."

Busy as she was, making sure Tremaine did not follow her or guess her intentions about the ship, several minutes passed before Marianna could review her conversation with the Frenchman.

Theirs had been a strange talk, to say the least. He had seemed to be digging for something—some piece of information—and at the same time threatening her. His decision to fire Harold, coming a full week before the time he had set for his answer, was another puzzle.

Something more kept pricking at the back of her consciousness. Marianna caught her breath. Tremaine had said he left Paris two years ago, but Christina Dowling had worked with him at the El Dorado in 1849. Besides, how had he known her sister lived in Oregon Territory? Could Harold have mentioned it? Harold couldn't have said anything about her uncle Ralph's and her brother-in-law's being pipe-smokers!

CHAPTER 12

WHO WAS JOHN TILTON? Was he Cole Taylor, as Gloriana suspected? Cole fit the description—charming and affluent. Moreover, he knew Applegate Landing, and he had practically probed for information about Gloriana. "Your rebel sister," he had called her and asked about her husband's work and whether Gloriana minded being left alone in her wilderness home.

Jacques Tremaine, on the other hand, did not fit the description, or did he? He was dark, of course, and some might find him charming: many women fell for the hand-kissing ploy. He did seem to know more about her family than he should, and he had lied about his arrival in San Francisco. But he could have any number of explanations for his information. Perhaps Harold talked about his relatives more than she realized; she might have read more into the man's words than was actually there; or it was even possible that he had been in Oregon Territory, had met Gloriana and Uncle Ralph. After all, Tremaine invested in gold mines, and there was gold in Oregon, wasn't there? He might have lied because he did not want anyone to know about his humble beginnings as a common gambler. Besides, the man was French. Gloriana had said nothing about John Tilton's having a French accent.

Face it, my dear, you are trying very hard to make a case where there is none and ignore the case that exists. Marianna sat back on her heels in front of the battered captain's table that she was using heated lemon oil and beeswax to restore. Much had happened in the week since she claimed salvage right to the beached clipper ship. A legal battle had been fought and won against the company that had managed the landfill. Since they had in effect beached the ship by surrounding it with sand, they had asserted a prior right to salvage. Christina Dowling's lawyer had countered with the information that public sand from the dunes north of the city had been used, making the fill a public beach and subject to public salvage. Then had come the work of cleaning and repairing the ship and hiring a staff for the shelter.

And throughout all those action-packed days, thoughts of the mysterious John Tilton had never been far from Marianna's mind; in fact, she had gone over her suspicions and half-suspicions so many times she couldn't tell a coincidence from a clue any longer and doubted she would recognize the missing piece of her puzzle if it were plopped down on the gleaming oak table in front of her.

It's always possible that neither man is Tilton, she reminded herself. *After all, 50,000 people are in San Francisco, most of them men. A large number are bound to have dark hair and brown eyes.*

The captain's cabin was the last part of the ship to be cleaned, and looking around her, Marianna felt a glow of satisfaction. The cabin, like the rest of the ship, gleamed. Six years of mildew had been removed from decks, hull, and walls. The scum of a thousand dank fogs had been scoured from portholes and hurricane lanterns. The rats had been banished from the hold and assorted spiders and insects from nooks and crannies. Below deck were curtains, rag carpets, brightly colored bedspreads, and frilled bolsters. Above deck, geraniums, daisies, marigolds, and fuchsias spilled from pots or kegs or boxes.

The ship had become an inviting home at only a fraction of the cost they had expected. The remainder of the $10,000 donated by Tremaine and the $20,000

Christina Dowling had expected to spend had been used to start a foundation. The future of the Chinatown Girls' Shelter would be secure. Marianna wished she felt as confident about her own future.

"My dear, you are scowling at that cleaning rag as though it had just bitten you. Don't tell me we missed some of those spiders after all." Christina Dowling, looking exquisite as usual in a black but modish gown, ducked to keep her bonnet from being crushed by the door frame. Behind her came Cole Taylor. His bent head just missed a collision, and he had to turn his broad shoulders sideways to get through the narrow doorway. In his arms were a tasseled pillow and a bouquet of ruby-hearted tea roses.

"Decorations for the new director's room," Christina explained. "Where should they go?"

Marianna reached for the pillow, then noticed with chagrin the oil and wax smeared on her hands, and pointed instead toward a low chair beside the table. She felt Cole's amused eyes on her and wished she could sink through the deck into the darkness of the hold. Her faded brown gingham dress had a rip at one elbow, was frayed around the hem and collar, and reeked from days of dusting, sweeping, scrubbing, and polishing. Her hair, which had started out in a neat bun, had worked its way loose and was poking from under her dust cap in stray wisps that stuck to her forehead and tickled her neck.

"Looking at the two of you, I would say someone hasn't been doing her share of the work," Cole accused playfully.

Marianna squirmed and started edging toward the door. It did not help at all for him to draw attention to her bedraggled state. But Christina made a face and laughed. "You're right. I've been perfectly useless; but this place will be a success in spite of me because of people like Marianna."

The admission melted the tiny barb of resentment Marianna had been harboring and reminded her once again of the widow's charm. Cole must have felt it too, for he laughed and called Christina the "Queen Bee," and a look passed between them so full of affectionate understanding that it made Marianna wince.

Mumbling something about having some supplies to check in the hold, she ducked out the door. Cole was obviously not breaking his heart over her. Once she was gone, he would turn to Christina as naturally as a sunflower to the sun. She tried to be glad; after all, she did like Christina; she was beautiful, rich, and a Christian. She would be perfect for Cole. *It's probably for the best.* Marianna reminded herself that "all things work together for good," but instead of feeling comforted, she felt very sad, and very, very lonely.

The hold had been partitioned off into classrooms, a meeting hall, and storerooms. Nothing needed her attention, but she lit a lantern and found her way into the maze of kegs, sacks, and boxes anyway.

"Marianna!" It was Cole's voice. She had not heard him follow her into the hold. For a minute she hesitated, then lifted her lamp so that it spotlighted her location.

"Why did you run off like that?"

To Marianna's over-sensitive ears he sounded more annoyed than concerned, and she snapped back. "Some of us have work to do. Besides, you had plenty to keep you busy, playing tame cat for the beautiful, rich widow." The words were spiteful and unjust, and Marianna wished them unsaid the moment they left her mouth.

In the lantern light Cole's angry face turned a menacing purple. He reached for her shoulders as though he would like to shake her, stood for a moment looking down into her frightened face, then let his hands drop back to his side with a little helpless gesture.

"Marianna, don't you find it a trifle inconsistent to be jealous of my friendship with Christina Dowling when you persist in your engagement to Harold Von Wooten?" His voice sounded both weary and exasperated.

He was right, of course. She had no right to object to anything he did. "That was unspeakable of me." Marianna caught her breath in a half-sob and blurted out a retraction. "I love Christina, really I do, and . . . and I believe she is the perfect woman for you. I know you will be happy together."

If she expected to see Cole's expression soften at her words, she was mistaken. His mouth remained set in a grim line, and the expression in his eyes made her shiver. Thinking he was feeling contempt for her half-apology, she tried again. "I am so sorry for acting like a jealous cat about Christina. She's wonderful."

"So wonderful that you're ready to give me up to her?"

The question startled Marianna, but she stammered out something that sounded like "yes."

"That's very noble of you." Cole had eliminated all expression from his tone. He looked away from her.

Marianna stepped forward and impulsively reached a hand toward him. "Please, I don't know what you want from me."

Cole shrugged away from her touch. "I want just two things from you, Marianna Windemere—honesty and trust. You seem unable to give me either."

Supporters of the Chinatown Girls' Shelter had scheduled the grand opening for a week after the staff began work on August 28. However, the shelter's work began quietly several days earlier.

The morning started badly. Marianna awakened late to a fogbound world and competing demands on her time. Some furniture was expected at the shelter, and she had promised to be there to supervise the unloading. She had barely managed to swallow a hot cup of tea and donned her plainest dress—though not a rag like the gingham Cole and Christina had caught her cleaning in—when Aunt Myriah demanded her company for another trip to Jacques Tremaine's office.

"We still have some unfinished business to take care of," Aunt Myriah reminded her with a meaningful glance toward the parlor. Tremaine had kept his promise about firing Harold, even to the extent of throwing him out of his rooms in the Tremaine Towers on Russian Hill. Harold had moved in with his stepmother and had spent most of the time since, brooding in the parlor, in his room upstairs, on the porch, in the back yard. Marianna dreaded the moment he discovered her aunt's role in his dismissal, as she had no doubt he would.

"You have some unfinished business," she corrected, guessing this trip had to do with the $20,000 and the Black Hills gold mine Aunt Myriah was to pay for Harold's release. Though the underhandedness of the method made Marianna squirm—too much like buying a human being—she could not help realizing Harold would be better off. He had been getting too involved in his boss's questionable business dealings. Imagine a Von Wooten involved in piracy! His blue-ribbon ancestors would be spinning in their graves.

Having set a time later in the day for the trip, Marianna hurried out the door, only to be stopped once again before she was out the gate this time by Mi Ling. The girl looked frightened. Her hands trembled as she thrust a note into Marianna's hand. The paper was limp and crumbly, as though it had been accidentally washed in someone's pocket.

"Father find in wash of bad man . . . one you remember." She motioned with her hands to indicate he had a hooked nose and jutting jaw. "Think you read English very well. Maybe tell meaning."

The note was in pencil and, therefore, still legible in spite of the dunking. The message was cryptic and unsigned:

Job for Dragon fire in Chinatown Aug 30 Corner CT—no slip-ups this time!

August 30, just a few days away! Whatever the job was, it had been tried unsuccessfully before; that was clear from the ominous "this time." But what was Dragon fire? And where was the corner of C and T? T might stand for Third Street, but what about C? Could it be a misspelling of Kearny, the busiest street in Chinatown?

"Should show it to Mr. Taylor?" Mi Ling tucked her hands in her sleeves to stop their trembling, but she could not control the anxiety that shaded her eyes black and made her seem pale in spite of her rich coloring. Preoccupied with her own fears, Marianna had forgotten how terrified Mi Ling must be of the thug who had tried to kidnap her.

Marianna started to ask Mi Ling to take the note to Cole's club but hesitated. Mi Ling had been humiliated the last time she had been forced to go there, and Marianna had learned enough about Oriental customs to know more was involved than a shy girl's embarrassment. For Mi Ling, visiting a men's club meant loss of face; in her world a calamity even more serious than losing one's reputation was in Marianna's. Moreover, they had no guarantee Cole Taylor would listen or even be interested. He had shrugged off her warnings before.

"No, we won't take it to Cole Taylor. I'll try to do something about it myself." She spoke with confidence, as though handling sinister plots were an everyday occurrence, but all the while she was sending out a quick S.O.S., *Help me, Lord.*

The morning fog looked thick and white from a distance yet dissolved close up into ragged see-through patches.

"It'll blow out of here by noon," assured the talkative streetcar driver. "Sure sign of a warm day inland when a fog bank rolls in. Heat sort of sucks it out of the ocean."

Certainly this fog was different from others Marianna had experienced in San Francisco. The mist felt smooth and powdery soft on her cheek, with none of the soaking chill or clammy dampness that preceded a coastal rainstorm.

By the time she reached the Girls' Shelter, a breeze had begun to tear the fog blanket into great ragged strips. White patches streamed like torn sails from her masts like the white caps of waves around her hull. The ship would have looked similar after a stormy night at sea—beaten but unbowed. How sad that a strong ship able to withstand storms at sea would never sail again, not because she was no longer seaworthy but because no one had been there to sail her on the tide. *The rest of her voyage of life will be "bound in shallows and miseries."* Marianna remembered the poem and her own fears the day the *Yankee Clipper* sailed.

Strangely enough, she no longer regretted not sailing from San Francisco. Although her months in that city had not been the happiest she had known, they had been the most alive. *For the first time I have really counted for something,* she thought, surveying the soon-to-be-opened shelter with a mixture of pride and awe. She may not have been the originator of the project, but, as Christina Dowling had said, she had contributed and that was what counted. Without a doubt the tide to be "taken at the flood" had been the one that brought her to San Francisco; now she must see whether it led on to fortune.

Like the captain of a ship, she sensed someone else on board the minute her foot touched the deck.

"Who's there?"

The remnants of the fog seemed to soften her voice and throw it back at her. It echoed down the deck of the empty ship.

"I can hear you. Come out, please."

Nothing to be afraid of. Nothing can happen in broad daylight. She looked up at the smoky disk glowing in the sky where the sun should be and willed bright golden rays to break through. *Why is it something that would not bother us in the sunshine scares us witless at night or in the fog?* Instinctively she grabbed a piece of driftwood that was part of the decorations and, holding it as menacingly as she could in front of her, edged along the deck toward the faint sound of whispers.

At the worst she expected some drunken miners who had stumbled on board to sleep off a night's carousing; at best, a gang of youngsters bent on mischief. She did not expect six sad-faced Chinese girls with the haunted eyes of old women, and three babies, so tiny and quiet they seemed more doll-like than human. They all looked at her with wide-eyed frightened expressions. Following the direction of their eyes, Marianna realized she was still brandishing the piece of driftwood and dropped it.

The clatter of the wood hitting the deck appeared to

break a spell, for all six women rose and bowed deeply. The leader came forward, tucking her hands neatly in her sleeves in the gesture Mi Ling so often used to disguise her trembling.

"We hear of shelter and come. See no one here. We go now."

"Go?" The word brought Marianna out of her stupor. For a cowardly moment she considered allowing the girls to leave. After all, wouldn't it be better for them to come back when trained personnel could help them, when people who spoke their own language could talk to them about their problems? Then she gave herself one of her swift mental kicks. The girls were obviously desperate but just as obviously terrified. It had probably taken all of their courage to come this morning; they might never make it back again.

"Please don't go! We're happy you came early. The shelter isn't scheduled for its grand opening until September 5, but that doesn't mean we're not open. We are! Open, I mean. And we're delighted you came." She knew she was babbling, but she hoped her chatter, however meaningless, would show she was friendly and at least wanted to help, even if she was not sure how to go about it.

What should she do first? What would she do first with any guest? Offer them something to eat!

Bustling now in a fair imitation of Aunt Myriah (though Marianna would have been horrified if she had realized it), she shepherded the little group into the cafeteria set up next to the galley. The storeroom had been stocked just the day before with items that would appeal to Chinese appetites. Marianna had only the vaguest ideas about cooking Chinese food, but she knew rice would take too long. Then she found something that looked like flour. With a few eggs and some brown sugar, she could serve them pancakes with syrup.

"Some people call them flapjacks," she went on explaining as she worked, "because of the way we flip-flap them over to brown the other side."

The girls listened politely and smiled politely, but their

appetites were anything but polite. Marianna nibbled on one of the pale cakes and made a little face—not absolutely terrible but not very tasty either. Certainly nothing she would want seconds of!

At least not unless she were starving, as these girls apparently were. It was astonishing that in the gold strike capital of the world people could be so hungry.

A little probing produced the information that all six girls worked in a Chinatown sweatshop where they wove intricate tapestries fourteen hours a day, seven days a week. Their wages amounted to no more than pennies because they were indentured—a condition that, in Chinatown at least, did not appear to place any obligations on the employer for food or shelter.

"Work night. That why we come here day," one younger girl, who by Marianna's guess could be no older than fourteen, explained carefully so that Marianna would know they were not shirking their responsibilities in coming to the shelter. Their quiet acceptance of their work and the injustices they suffered reminded Marianna of Mi Ling's attitude about being a maid at the hotel. Probably they also knew of too many worse fates to complain about their own.

She offered them rooms to rest in, but the girls' spokeswoman—probably the one who knew the most English—said they must return to their families. Still, they promised to come again and even giggled a little at Marianna's effusive invitations to eat, visit the doctor, study English and, most importantly, learn about Jesus in Bible classes.

"You're wasting your time, you know." The harsh words cut roughly into Marianna's dreams. Standing at the foot of the gangplank, Harold threw a contemptuous look after the Chinese girls. His sneer extended to Marianna and the lovely old ship as he lounged on board, his hands in his pockets and his top hat, badly in need of brushing, cocked over his eyebrow.

"Isn't it rather early in the day to be drinking?" she asked coldly.

"Shows how much you know, Miss Goody-Two-

Shoes. I haven't been drinking, though I do have a hangover." He laughed and threw himself down on the edge of a flower box, crushing a petunia in the process.

"That's the trouble with you pure-of-heart ladies. You think you know so much . . . always poking your noses in where they're not wanted. Well, I can tell you this: your little attempt at mercy is doomed before it starts. If the girls' families don't put a stop to it, the Dragon will."

Marianna's breath caught in her throat and she nearly gasped, "What do you mean? Who is the Dragon?"

"Scares you, doesn't it?" Harold sneered his satisfaction. "The Dragon is the leader of the toughest gang of thugs in San Francisco, and from what I hear he doesn't think much of you and your friends and your do-gooding in Chinatown."

CHAPTER 13

SAN FRANCISCO HAD NO POLICE DEPARTMENT, but the city did have a marshal, a few deputies, and a jail too small to have served a town a third the size and a hundred times more law-abiding.

Marianna was kept waiting ten minutes before she could give Mi Ling's ominous washtub-soaked note to an harassed deputy, so busy with a stack of wanted posters that he barely gave her a glance.

"We'll do what we can, ma'am. We've heard of the Dragon." He was sympathetic but somehow relayed the impression the threat would have been taken more seriously if it had involved any part of the city other than Chinatown. "You've got to realize, ma'am, these things happen every day down there." Remembering the Fourth of July assassination, she believed him.

The memory also brought back a vivid picture of the parade dragon and the sinister man with the gun—heavy jaw, thick lips set in a scowl, nose with a break in the middle that bent it back in a pronounced hook. She described the man to the deputy and added, "He could be the Dragon. I've been told he works for Jacques Tremaine."

The deputy's eyes flew to her face at that. She could

not tell whether he was startled by the information or by her giving it to him. "If you're sure about that, we might be able to find him," was all the deputy said, but Marianna could sense that he did not like what he had heard.

Harold, who had accompanied her to the jail, had been suspicious when they went in; he was furious when they came out.

"Are you crazy? You just informed on one of the most dangerous men in San Francisco!" Anger brought color to Harold's pasty complexion. The hand that grabbed her arm was shaking.

"Which man do you mean, Harold, the Dragon or your exemployer?" She met his eyes squarely.

"Both! Haven't you enough sense to know you can't fight men like that?"

"Are you saying it's better to look the other way when I might be able to prevent a disaster? Am I supposed to forget about right and wrong just because of some element of risk? I didn't go looking for that information. It came to me accidentally, but once it did, I had a moral obligation to tell the authorities about it."

Harold flushed and dropped her arm. "You don't understand. Things are different here than back East. Sometimes a man doesn't have any choice but to look the other way."

Guilt, fear, defiance—all were mixed in Harold Von Wooten's expression. A bright ray of sun, breaking through the fog now rolling rapidly inland, spotlighted his face, setting off the pale hair with its slight wave over his forehead, the long white eyelashes, and drooping mustache. A blond stubble of unshaved whiskers was visible on his chin and cheeks. The eyelids were heavy, the blue eyes shot with spiderwebs of tiny blood vessels. Dark shadows lurked under his eyes, and deep lines were etched from nose to mouth. His was, Marianna decided, a weak face, perhaps always had been. The West, she had read somewhere, either made or broke men. Harold was one it had broken.

"If a man looks the other way too many times, he

becomes a party to the injustice. He's already stepped over the line. From there to taking an active part is a small step."

"What do you mean by that?" He sounded defiant but scared too.

"I'm guessing, Harold, but I wouldn't be surprised if you looked the other way from your employer's questionable business methods too many times. When he finally asked you to do something illegal as well as immoral—like ramming Cole Taylor's steamship—you didn't have much choice."

"Better watch it, Marianna. You're sounding more like Myriah every day," Harold growled, but his face told her what she wanted to know. "While you're at it, why don't you do some of that preaching to your good *friend,* Taylor. He's been involved in plenty of shady deals in his time."

Marianna took a deep breath and forced herself not to answer. She couldn't change Harold. When they had arrived in San Francisco, she had felt she was meeting a new Harold, but perhaps he was just thc old one—the real person who had been hidden inside the masks painted by family associations and society—who had been given a chance to grow.

"Harold, do you still consider yourself a Christian?" she asked him suddenly.

He hesitated, probably as taken aback by her question as Marianna was herself. Von Wootens, like Windemeres, were always Christians. "If you want to know whether I have given up on church these last few years, I suppose I have. But that doesn't mean that I won't go when we get back home. I know what's expected."

"I didn't ask you if you went to church. I asked if you were a Christian."

He looked embarrassed now and shrugged. "I'll leave that part to you women." He laughed and an unpleasant smirk crossed his face. "You won't catch me going to prayer breakfasts and witnessing on street corners. You won't catch me taking the pledge and becoming a sissy teetotaler either. Why, your friend Taylor and his '49ers are the laughingstock of San Francisco."

Marianna swung around and grabbed his arm. They were in the middle of Union Square, and several passersby stared at them curiously, but she did not care.

"What do you mean?"

Harold's smile was sly and malicious. "Surprises you, doesn't it? I'll bet you thought you had hooked yourself to a western he-man like Gloriana's Graham Norton. Everyone knows you have to make what they call a Christian commitment to belong to the '49ers, and it makes for a pretty dull club, if you ask me. Rumor even has it that what Cole packs under his black coat—you know, where it bulges—is not a shoulder holster but a Bible."

Marianna's eyes flashed. She had spots of color in her cheeks, and her dark curls bounced with every indignant shake of her head. "For your information, Harold Von Wooten, the only real he-men are Christians. They have the only kind of courage that matters—the courage of their convictions. Furthermore, don't think for one minute that a pampered, spoiled Harvard-boy from Philadelphia can tell someone like Cole Taylor what it takes to be a man. He has more true manliness in his little finger than you have in your whole body!"

A ripple of applause greeted Marianna's outburst. Looking around she found herself at the center of an appreciative crowd. From their whole-hearted approval, she gathered that Cole was popular and Harold, if anyone here even knew him, was not.

Red-faced and feeling, to her mortification, she was developing Aunt Myriah's knack for making a scene in public, Marianna left Harold standing in the middle of Union Square.

Why hadn't Cole told her he was a Christian? Or, more importantly, why hadn't she known? His words, his actions, his way of living, even his ways of loving—all pointed to someone who was part of the family of God. She had been so busy looking for what she expected to see that she had missed what was actually in front of her. She had expected Harold to be a Christian because he came from her hometown and her home church and he was part of her own family. She had expected Cole Taylor not to be a Christian because he called himself a San Franciscan and because he carried with him that aggressive excitement, that western spirit or vision or fever she had distrusted and feared. Moreover, it was obvious that Gloriana's suspicions were absurd. Cole couldn't be John Tilton; she didn't need any other evidence.

But now what was she going to do about it? Cole was angry because she had not trusted him and he thought she was playing games. Aunt Myriah, and probably Harold too, would want to be returning home. She couldn't stay without them, yet she couldn't bear the thought of going. She loved the beauty of San Francisco Bay, the specialness of this mushroom city with its sedate Philadelphia-style streets transformed by steep hills into roller coasters, its exotic mingling of races and cultures, Chinatown, the busy wharves, the avenue of beached ships, Telegraph Hill with its clear view of the fabulous Golden Gate. But most of all, she loved Cole Taylor.

Please work it out, Lord. I can't leave him, but I can't stay unless he asks me. Someone once called you the God-of-one-more-chance. I need that chance.

The afternoon was devoted to finding Jacques Tremaine. Harold had caught up with her before Marianna had reached home, so no embarrassing explanations about returning by herself were needed. Yet Marianna sensed a constraint in her aunt's manner, a barely submerged agitation that grew as they traveled from Tremaine's Market Street office to his home down the peninsula and finally to the El Dorado, where he was reportedly engaged in a high-stakes card game.

"Marianna, I don't know what my brother would say if he knew I took you into a place like this, but I have no choice. I can't leave you alone outside with so many men coming and going. You'll just have to stay close to me and keep your eyes down. Don't talk to anyone. Don't look at anyone. We'll just slip in and out again before anyone notices."

For two prim ladies to slip in and out of the El Dorado without being noticed was about as possible as for a lamb to walk unnoticed through a lion's den. Heads turned. Glasses were left poised in midair. The piano player stopped playing. The roulette wheel, however, kept spinning.

Forgetting her aunt's warning to keep her eyes down, Marianna looked around her with lively curiosity. The room was larger and lighter than she had imagined. Somehow she had supposed gamblers and drinkers would require small, dimly lit rooms for their activities. The ground floor at least of the El Dorado was gas-lit by huge, multi-tiered chandeliers, and the light was intensified by mirrors running the length of the bar. She looked at, then glanced quickly away from the pictures of women in various states of undress that hung over the bar.

How, she wondered, *could the women who work here appear so nonchalant?* At least five women were in the room—all heavily made up and wearing dresses that plunged at the neckline and soared at the hemline. She caught a glimpse of their eyes—hard, with that old-young look that went straight to her heart. She could not imagine Christina Dowling among them. Here was certainly another ripe field for that reforming San Francisco matron.

Men in all styles of dress were drinking at the bar or gambling at an assortment of roulette and fortune wheels, card and dice tables. Prospectors in corduroys and suspenders jostled against gentlemen in cutaway coats and frilled shirts. All seemed very intense about their activities. What laughter she heard was coarse and raucous. If this was a "pleasure palace," as Cole had told her, no one seemed to be having a very good time.

As if to keep them from coming further into the casino, a man wearing a red coat and an officious manner—obviously the manager—hurried toward them.

"What can I do for you ladies?" he asked, but his tone and lifted eyebrows said, "Please leave!"

Aunt Myriah gathered herself to her full height, which,

if not great, at least seemed so with her towering bonnet and high-heeled, high-button boots. She looked down her nose and demanded in her most imperious tone, "Show me to Jacques Tremaine immediately."

The man looked as though he would like to argue but, after a moment's assessment, shrugged and led the way through the curious crowd.

"Probably decided the easiest way to get rid of us was to give in," Marianna whispered to her aunt.

Aunt Myriah gave her a cold stare that said more clearly than words, "This is not a game, Marianna."

Tremaine was playing cards in a back parlor that reeked of stale cigar smoke. He and the other men in the game were in their shirt-sleeves with their cuffs rolled back and ties loosened or gone. One man stood to put on his coat when he saw the ladies at the door, but most, including Tremaine, just glared at them over the tops of their cards and went on playing.

"Mr. Tremaine," the manager was nervous but insistent, "these ladies would not leave until they spoke with you."

Tremaine scowled at the cards in his hand and at the short stack of chips in front of him, then laughed. "I'll have to sit this hand out, boys."

Marianna's eyes widened in surprise and interest. Was it her imagination, or had those words been remarkably free of accent? She thought she saw a sardonic gleam in the eyes that met hers. When he spoke again, his speech was peppered with French and even more heavily accented than usual.

"*Excusez-moi, madame, mademoiselle,* it has been such a long game; I forget my manners." He escorted them to a little office at the end of the hall. Remembering he had worked at the El Dorado as a dealer before he became a wealthy entrepreneur, Marianna wondered whether he owned an interest in the place. Her question was answered a moment later when he opened the safe beside the desk and took out a white envelope.

"*Je regrette* the necessity of seeing you here. It is not *peut-être* a place for ladies such as yourselves. However, one cannot predict the length of a card game. This one has been going on for forty-eight hours. But to business, as you Americans say. I have decided to change the conditions of our *petite* arrangement *un soupçon*."

Aunt Myriah's face turned an angry red and she sputtered, "I only sent for the items we discussed; it will take months to get more."

Tremaine raised his hand to stop the stream of protests and handed her the white envelope. "I have added only one condition—that is for you and your family to leave San Francisco immediately. Tickets are in the envelope for the steamer *Atlantis*. She sails on August 30 for Panama." He smiled mockingly at Marianna, and the light in his eyes made her shudder. She wondered how she could ever have thought him handsome. "Mademoiselle Windemere will no doubt find it *tres̄ difficile* to tear herself away from her good works and, if I may say so, from a certain San Francisco *gentilhomme*. But I'm sure she will find Philadelphia just as much in need of her efforts.

"And now I believe it is time for you to give something to me, *n'est-ce pas*?"

If Aunt Myriah were reluctant to turn over $20,000 and her gold mine, she did not show it. Tremaine laughed at the deed and joked about using it to make another start if he lost his shirt in the card game. He put the deed in the safe but took the cash, two large stacks of bills, back to the smoke-filled room. His eyes lingered a moment on Marianna. "I wish, *ma chérie*, that we had had the opportunity for a, shall we say, 'closer' acquaintance. Perhaps in another time and another place."

Both ladies breathed sighs of relief when they had left the glittering, brittle atmosphere of the El Dorado behind them.

"Marianna, I think we were very fortunate to get your cousin away from that man. It would have been worth it at any price."

"The real trick, though, will be to change Harold back the way he was before Jacques Tremaine came into his life."

The old lady gave Marianna a shrewd look. "That may be a lifelong battle; and something tells me that you have better things to do with your life." She reached into her reticule and pulled out a small envelope. "This came for you this morning. I've been debating ever since whether to give it to you. I can tell a man's handwriting when I see it, and you and Harold are way past the stage of love letters. I suppose it's from that Cole Taylor you think so much of."

But it wasn't. The unmistakably masculine hand was unfamiliar—a sharply slanted scrawl rather than Cole's firm up-and-down letters.

Marianna tore open the envelope and found the return address inside.

Applegate Landing
Oregon Territory
August 7, 1855

My dear sister,

Gloriana has just told me about her letter to you, and I am following it with one of my own to clear up a misunderstanding.

Gloriana was right to worry about your meeting John Tilton in San Francisco. I have heard he is there, is frequently seen at the El Dorado, and is more evil than before. But he is not Cole Taylor.

I have met Taylor more than once on my trips to Eureka. He is a fine, Christian man, and, if you are, as Gloriana implies, falling in love with him, you have our blessing.

Gloriana says she urged you to find out who John Tilton is. Don't. The man is much too dangerous, and he would not hesitate to harm you if he thought by doing so he would hurt Gloriana. He was more than halfway in love with her. I am told that the army is on his trail and an investigator will soon be in San Francisco. Until then, forget you ever heard about John Tilton.

Affectionately, your brother-in-law,
Graham Norton

"Well, are you going to tell me who is writing to my niece behind my back?"

"It's not behind your back, aunt, and it's not Cole Taylor." *But I wish it were,* Marianna added to herself. Why hadn't she trusted him when she had the chance?

CHAPTER 14

THEY WERE LEAVING SAN FRANCISCO AT LAST, and Harold was going with them. Just a few short weeks before, Marianna would have been triumphant; now she felt as though her life would be over when the *Atlantis* steamed out through the Golden Gate.

"But you can't go! What about our work with the Girls' Shelter? What about the needlework lessons you were going to give? What about the fund drives, the foundation board? You're to be secretary. We need you here in San Francisco." Christina Dowling's distress was genuine, and the knowledge she would be missed by this woman she had resented as a rival made Marianna feel at once grateful and ashamed. How often had she felt or said unkind things about Christina? Now the thought she might never see the lonely widow again brought tears to Marianna's eyes.

"It's not that I want to go," she tried to explain. "I just don't have a choice." She looked longingly around the parlor of her aunt's rented house, then out the window at the by-now familiar panorama of sloping hills, docked ships, and blue water. "I don't want to go," she repeated, and her voice broke.

Christina ran to her and put an arm around Marianna's

shoulders. "Perhaps I shouldn't say this, but have you talked it over with Cole? Does he know you are leaving? I think it will break his heart."

"But with me gone, I thought you and he would . . . that is, nothing would stand in the way of . . ." She couldn't finish.

Christina's eyes widened in amazement. "You don't mean you thought Cole and I were romantically involved? My dear, he's like a brother to me!"

"You're so close, I thought you cared about each other."

"Of course, we care about each other. He was my husband's dearest friend. We're like family." A look of indecision passed over Christina's face, then she shrugged her shoulders. "Cole would be furious if he knew I was telling you this, but do you know what he said to me the day you all landed on the *Yankee Clipper*? He said, 'Christina, I've finally found the right girl. She doesn't know it yet, but I'm not going to let her go back to Philadelphia.' That's why I was stunned when I met you and you introduced this Harold person as your fiancé."

The way she said "this Harold person" sounded so exactly like Aunt Myriah that ordinarily Marianna would have laughed or at least smiled a little, but she did not hear. Her mind was on Cole's words. They were bittersweet, reminding her of what she had lost at the same time that they confirmed what had been hers.

"That was before I treated him so badly," she admitted at last, and with her breath on the edge of a sob, Marianna choked out the story of her suspicions, her jealousies, the games she had been playing with Cole and with herself over the past few weeks. By the time she had finished, Christina looked thoroughly exasperated, but affection as well as annoyance was behind her scolding.

"How could you possibly think Cole might be such a monstrous villain? If I were going to suspect anyone, it would be Jacques. He was gone from San Francisco at the right time; he came back incredibly rich; I can't believe he worked for his money. Moreover, he is capable of anything vile. Believe me, I know." Christina's face clouded for a moment; she shook off the gloom and brought her words back determinedly to her friend's problems.

"I still think your best bet is to tell Cole you don't want to go back home. Trust him to work out a solution. If he wants you to do penance for a while, you can stay with me until you get married. We could even make a job for you at the shelter so the gossips can't say you're camping on Cole's trail."

I've finally found the right girl. Marianna kept saying those words to herself after Christina left, savoring them, trying to imagine the half-grin on Cole's face and the teasing light in his eyes as he said them. Finally, her courage boosted and an it's-now-or-never determination on her face, she went to her writing desk and took out a sheet of stationery. Hardly giving herself time to think, she filled a page with her aunt's plans, her own wish to stay in San Francisco, and hints about her true feelings for him. It took her last silver dollar and a piece of Aunt Myriah's chocolate cake to convince the neighbor boy to deliver the note to the '49ers volunteer fire station.

To keep calm, she packed while she waited for a reply, all the while hoping she could unpack it all again when she heard from Cole. She half expected him to come in person. After all, hadn't he said he wouldn't let her go back to Philadelphia, and wasn't he the kind of man who did what he said?

Instead, the neighbor returned with a note and, Marianna had no doubt, something larger than her silver dollar in his pocket. The message was brief and to the point.

Dear Marianna,

I understand how you feel about leaving San Francisco. I couldn't stand to go myself.

But things are happening right now that make it better for you to leave. I'm not saying I won't miss you, but I'll rest easier knowing you're safe.

I'll be in Philadelphia myself in the spring. I hope you won't marry Harold—or anyone else!—until I get there.

In the meantime, don't argue. Just go. I'll explain everything in a letter.

Yours as always,
Cole

P.S. I would go to the docks to see you off, but Harold wouldn't like it.

Not much in the tone or words made her feel he cared about her, yet it was not a final good-by either. He would be coming to Philadelphia in the spring. He said he would miss her, or at least he almost said it. "Yours as always" could mean he hadn't changed his feelings about her; his heart was still hers. The mention of Harold sounded jealous, and of course, he was still bossing her around. He wouldn't do that if he had lost interest completely.

"But it puts me back where I started—waiting in Philadelphia!" Marianna was appalled. She started to say, "You can't do this to me, Lord," but remembered in time that she had promised to stop tempting and start trusting. Yet her heart sank at the prospect of months, perhaps years of waiting, this time without anything solid to hold onto. She wasn't even engaged to Cole.

"It looks as if my tide didn't lead on to fortune," she told herself gloomily and set about preparing to leave in earnest.

She had more to do than packing and saying good-by. Household articles borrowed from acquaintances around the city must be returned. Aunt Myriah had seen a silk screen in Chinatown and decided at the last minute she could not live without it; it had to be found and purchased. Gifts of clothes and toiletries must be left at the shelter; a farewell tea at the Dowling mansion must be prepared for and endured; and even instructions must be left with a local attorney about a small investment Aunt Myriah had made. "Nothing risky like a gold mine," she had explained. "Nothing combustible like this wooden house either—too many fires for that. I invested in the one thing that will soar in value over the next few years—land on Nob Hill." They were too short of time to visit Aunt Myriah's acres, but seen over the rooftops they looked rather desolate. Nonetheless, Marianna remembered that it was largely her aunt's business sense that had made the Von Wooten fortune; no doubt she knew, as usual, what she was doing.

Harold did not get in their way, but he did not help either. He had accumulated surprisingly little during his three years in San Francisco; that little was soon boxed and ready to be hauled to the docks. If he had friends to say good-by to, he must have done it in writing, for he rarely left the house even to sit on the porch or buy a paper. Marianna was the one who ran to Chinatown for her aunt, who went to the docks to make arrangements for someone to haul their trunks, who carried an armload of dresses, some of them her favorites, to the Girls' Shelter.

"I may have lost rather than gained a son through what I've done," Aunt Myriah confided in Marianna.

She disagreed. Far from being reluctant to leave, Harold now seemed eager. "He doesn't know what you did. And even if he did know, I think he's beginning to realize this place is not right for him. He wouldn't have lasted much longer."

San Francisco was not right for Harold, but it was right for Mi Ling. From the moment she had heard about Marianna's leaving, she had assumed she would go also. "My place is with you," she had said with a quiet dignity that could not wholly cover her distress at leaving her family and friends.

Taking an indentured Chinese servant home with her was, of course, impossible. Marianna had never heard of anyone's being excommunicated from her father's church, but she was sure that if it were possible, a minister's daughter who owned a Chinese slave would be a likely candidate. But how could she leave Mi Ling and still protect her?

That problem was foremost in Marianna's mind as she hurried down Sacramento Avenue on another errand for her aunt.

The avenue was crowded with traffic. Carriages jostled against freight wagons. Street cars rolled noisily along, their bells clanging and their conductors calling out destinations, "Market Street," "Chinatown," "Telegraph Hill," "Steamship Wharf," "Clipper Wharf," "Fisherman's Wharf." Around her on the boardwalk pedestrians held onto their hats to protect them from gusts. Equal numbers of people with and without umbrellas attested to the unsettled state of the weather—cloudy one moment, sunshiny the next.

Marianna felt Cole before she saw him. He was wearing his usual frock coat, open over an embroidered vest, and a black hat, tilted back on his head. He was talking to a plump red-cheeked woman whose Dutch cap and apron proclaimed her the owner of the nearby cruller and doughnut shop. As though he felt her eyes on him, Cole turned and waved, but he did not smile. Marianna looked quickly in another direction, while out of the corner of her eye she saw him hesitate, then tip his hat to the shopkeeper, and dart through the traffic toward her side of the street.

"Why aren't you home packing?" The abrupt question brought Marianna's startled eyes to his, and Cole colored at the wistful reproach he saw there.

"I'm running an errand for Aunt Myriah. I didn't think I would see you before I left."

Cole mumbled something that sounded like "the flesh is weak," cleared his throat, then lost whatever he had been about to say as an errant gust lifted his hat from its precarious perch on the back of his head and flung it down a steep alley. By the time they had chased it behind a row of false-fronted buildings, across a yard hung, fence-to-fence, with lines of clean wash flapping in the wind, and finally corralled it, floating in a fresh-water cistern atop the roof of a painter's shop, the constraints were gone, and they were laughing and holding onto each other trying to get their breath.

The hat was battered but not beyond recognition. Its flat crown and narrow brim sagged. The crown had been dented and somewhere the black felt had acquired a giant smudge of glaring yellow paint.

"Could be useful if I wanted to spot it in the dark." Cole dabbed at the paint with his handkerchief, managing to smear the color further.

Marianna giggled. "Remove the paint with turpentine, and the smell will guide you to it, even if you can't see it in the dark."

They sank weakly to a flight of steps between terraced gardens. Above them the steps climbed at a nearly ninety-degree angle toward houses perched on the hill-side. Below, the steps cut back and forth from garden to garden until they emerged into a busy street. The sounds of the traffic were muffled by the buildings—a distant backdrop of shouts, clanging street cars, and wheels rolling over board planks.

For the space of a breath, their glances met and held.

Cole broke the silence, his voice roughened by emotion. "Don't think me a beast for not coming to you. I understand what you were trying to say in your letter, but it's not the right time. I have enemies. You wouldn't be safe with me now."

Marianna kept her eyes on his face. The clean, strong lines inspired confidence as well as admiration, but she saw signs of care and worry she had not seen there before—little creases at the center of the forehead, a tenseness about the mouth that turned the corners down rather than up, a determined set to the jaw as though he were gritting his teeth in a time of trouble.

"Will I be truly safe on ship in stormy autumn seas or traveling across Panama? I won't know a moment's peace worrying about what is happening to you here and wondering whether I will ever see you again."

With a sigh Cole reached for her, glanced down at the ever-present pearl on her left hand, and pressed her upturned face against his shoulder.

"Marianna, if we are meant to be together, the Lord will work something out. We just have to trust him."

Trusting when you can't see a clear path to the answer was, Marianna decided, like walking blindfolded through a room strewn with obstacles. You scrape your knees and bump your shins, but eventually, if you keep on going, you can hope to find a door.

Marianna felt bruised and wondered vaguely whether she were going in circles as the hours passed and August 30, the day set for the *Atlantis* to sail, drew closer.

Tea at Christina Dowling's Park Place mansion was spent taking messages from homesick San Francisco matrons to be delivered to friends and families back East. Christina managed to whisper a quick question, "Did you tell Cole?" But Marianna only had time to answer, "He wants me to go." She was glad they had no time for a lengthy discussion; she could feel the tears pricking at her eyelids and knew it would not take much to set her sobbing.

She considered appealing to Christina to take Mi Ling, but before she had a chance, her prayers for the Chinese girl were answered to everyone's satisfaction. The sound of voices outside the kitchen drew Marianna down the stairs and out the screen door to the porch. Mi Ling was standing on the steps, her hands folded firmly into her sleeves and her eyes fixed intently on the ground at the feet of the Chinese vegetable merchant. He was speaking in Chinese, but the passion and earnestness of his tone said he was pleading with her about something.

"Is everything all right?" The startled, embarrassed looks turned her way made it obvious that Marianna had interrupted a discussion of something more personal than the price of an ear of corn or a cabbage.

"Everything fine," Mi Ling hurried to assure her. "My friend Wu Ton Chow just leaving."

But he did not leave. Instead, he bowed respectfully to Marianna and launched into an explanation of his status as a naturalized citizen, the prosperity of his truck farm, and the kindness of his mother and two sisters, who lived with him. "Most important," he concluded in English much clearer than Mi Ling's, "I am like Mi Ling, a Christian."

Bewildered, Marianna said something about being impressed or pleased or happy for him, while she looked to Mi Ling for an explanation.

Mi Ling surprised her by turning a deep dusky red and glaring angrily at the man. "I tell him I must go with you, but he not listen. Want to marry me now, keep me here."

It was the perfect solution. Beaming, Marianna seized and shook Wu Ton Chow's hand and drew him into the kitchen. Ordinarily Marianna did not approve of arranged marriages, but she could tell in spite of Mi Ling's angry protests that the girl loved her vegetable farmer. So amid the clutter on the kitchen table, Marianna for the first and only time arranged a marriage. The papers of indenture were unearthed from her trunk, read, and signed so that Wu Ton Chow would be not only Mi Ling's husband, but also her sponsor. Then Mi Ling's family was sent for from Chinatown and the minister from the church. And in the garden, overlooking the bay, Mi Ling married Wu Ton Chow.

"Now I feel you will be safe," Marianna told the bride as she hugged her.

"But I miss you," Mi Ling whispered back. "Maybe you marry Mr. Taylor and stay too."

To everyone's amazement, Aunt Myriah entered into the full spirit of the activities by having a wedding dinner catered by an uptown restaurant and wrapping a present for the newlyweds.

"Hard to get started in this town with the prices what they are," the old lady said gruffly. And in a box of practical white linen sheets with double pillow cases and embroidery threads to be used in decorating them, the couple found ten twenty-dollar gold pieces.

Even Harold managed to come up with a gift. From somewhere in his bags, he pulled a pair of white silk Mandarin robes and matching slippers. Doves, exquisitely embroidered in gold thread, edged the stand-up collar and bordered the sleeves and hem.

"Why, they look like wedding robes!" Marianna exclaimed delightedly. She started to ask Harold how he happened to have such beautiful garments in his possession, then thought better of it.

"I don't think I'll be needing them now," he said with a bleak look at Marianna, but he seemed genuinely pleased with the Chinese couple's awed reactions.

Marianna had a harder time with her gift. Her spending money was gone, but she did have a beautiful jade cross on an intricate gold chain that she could give the bride. For the groom, she found a shop where she could exchange her favorite *Pilgrim's Progress* for a Chinese New Testament.

To top off the festivities, the bride's brothers brought strings of firecrackers to set off in the garden. The sparks from the lighted fuses jumped and glowed in the dark like nervous fireflies, and the popping echoed from the hilltop.

Finally, the last congratulation had been said and the last best wishes given. The happy couple took their gifts and Mi Ling's small roll of possessions and departed for the bridegroom's farm, followed merrily by the brothers and their firecrackers.

"Marianna, I didn't understand that business about indentures and your gift of some papers."

"It isn't important, Aunt Myriah. We'll talk about it later."

"Something tells me you don't intend to talk about it ever, but I won't pry. Something also tells me that I do entirely too much of that."

Marianna lingered on the porch, watching the full moon riding over a gleaming silver bay. The air was scented with roses and tinged with the faint salty taste of a sea breeze. Below, the city's gaslights outlined the pattern of streets and cross-streets and formed a border for the clusters of lights beaming into the darkness from open windows or glowing softly behind closed curtains.

"You'll miss it, won't you?" Harold stood beside her at the porch rail.

"More than I would have thought possible."

He started to reach for her hand, but she moved it away.

"When you came here two months ago, you wanted nothing more than for us three to go home again. Now I have the feeling you want nothing more than to stay."

Marianna did not answer but folded her arms tightly around her to warm herself against the night chill.

"I wish I could say everything will look different back East, and we'll soon find nothing has changed," she said softly, "but that's not true. You've changed. I've changed. You know I can't marry you now, don't you?"

Harold cleared his throat to speak, tried, but couldn't, and settled for nodding his head.

"We never were right for each other." Her voice was wistful as she remembered regretfully lost dreams and the lost years of waiting.

"You're wrong, Marianna. You were right for me. I just wasn't the right man for you."

She hardly realized when Harold left the porch. Her thoughts were on the man who was right for her but was determined to send her back to Philadelphia while he stayed in San Francisco. *We sail tomorrow, Lord. You're running out of time!*

CHAPTER 15

THE *ATLANTIS* WOULD NOT PUT TO SEA until midnight. The steamship would hug the coasts of California and Mexico until it reached Panama. Then the passengers would board the new railroad, just completed a few weeks earlier, to cross the isthmus and meet the East Coast steamer waiting in the Caribbean.

The steamers, sturdy and reliable, kept strictly to schedule, and their coastal route, usually within sight of land, provided an extra margin of safety. Squat, uncomfortable, and decidedly unpicturesque, their hulls were shaped like flat back-to-back wedges, pointed at the bow and stern. The draft was shallow, poised on the surface of the water to allow the ship to navigate rivers as well as the sea and destined to make seasick passengers feel every wave and swell. Short masts—a precaution in case the engines should fail—sat fore and aft, but the engine house and enclosed wheel occupied most of the midship area. The few cabins below deck were tiny, and little space was found above for passengers.

Supervising the loading of their baggage, Marianna visualized the weeks they would spend in these cramped, dismal quarters and prayed again for a last-minute reprieve. Jacques Tremaine had certainly not considered their comfort when he purchased their tickets; in fact, his main consideration appeared to have been speed. The voyage on a clipper would take nearly three months; the steamers and railroad trip across Panama reduced that by half.

Marianna remembered sailing gloriously through the Golden Gate on the *Yankee Clipper* and was glad the *Atlantis* would make its more pedestrian exit at night. She did not want the memory of chugging stolidly through that portal to blot out the picture of a tall ship leaning into the wind, its masts filled with white sails, sweeping grandly between the towering golden bluffs of the Gate.

She was glad too that the ship would get underway directly from the dock, leaving no need to board early and put out into the bay to wait for the tide. Every delay was a chance for something to happen.

After the hectic activity of the past days, their last hours in San Francisco seemed empty. They had said their good-bys, so no friends were left to call on. Their luggage was on board, the larger trunks in the hold and only small bags in their cabins, so they would have no place to put their purchases if they shopped. Even Mi Ling was gone, enjoying her first day as the wife of Wu Ton Chow. The rented kitchen was ominously silent without her melodious sing-song voice trilling over her chores, or her quick tiny steps skipping over the bare wood floor.

Marianna was silent and her feet dragged as she took Mi Ling's place preparing the day's meals and washing the day's dishes. The lovely china Aunt Myriah's friends had loaned her had been returned, and in its place they used heavy, chipped blue pottery left by the owner of the house. The thick-rimmed cups made the savory jasmine tea seem tasteless, and even the delicate leftovers of shaved ham and spiced hors d'oeuvres from Mi Ling's wedding party seemed like coarse fare on cracked plates.

They had no view from the kitchen windows, and Marianna avoided the parlor where Harold and Aunt Myriah waited out the day. As she worked at the sink, pumping water to be heated on the stove or preparing a hamper to take on board with them—they might need the extra food—she could see the sky change from the high gray fog of early morning, to the metal blue of midday, to the softer, cloud-streaked turquoise of afternoon. The coast winds, little more than sea breezes in the morning, picked up in the afternoon and sent clotted-cream clouds scuttling across the westerly sun. The sky was filled with birds—winging flights of gulls and terns riding the winds from the ocean, fish hawks silhouetted against the sun, and closer at hand, mud swallows dipping and swooping around eaves of houses, and hummingbirds dressed in ruby and emerald feathers darting from flower to flower in the garden.

As she watched, a gull that had been sunning itself on a nearby roof sprang into the air. Its wings gleamed white, then caught the slanting sun with a violet glow. The bird soared higher and higher into the western sky until its broad wings were no more than a tiny moving V. Marianna recalled the lines of a poem "To a Waterfowl," she had once worked into a sampler. The needlework had been dark blue, the color of hope, on a light blue background—hope upon hope, she had called it.

There is a Power whose care
Teaches thy way along that pathless coast,—
The desert and illimitable air,
Lone wandering, but not lost.
He, who, from zone to zone,
Guides through the boundless sky thy certain flight,
In the long way that I must trace alone,
Will lead my steps aright.

They had lingered over a dinner of cold chicken and bread without really tasting it and were gathering their wraps to start for the wharf when the chilling clang of the firebell began its toll. One, two, three tolls followed by a rolling peal that meant volunteers were needed at a three-alarm fire, not a crisis but serious enough in a city that had burned nearly to the water six times in its six-year history.

From the porch, they scanned the city for the spark of flames or a column of smoke. To the west the sun had set in the ocean, leaving the horizon ablaze with orange, yellow, and red lights. Behind it the city was sinking into a purple twilight that disguised smoke with shadows.

"There it is!" Harold pointed toward a billowing gray cloud halfway between the wharves and Telegraph Hill. A glint of flames was visible at its base before a gust of wind swept across the city, leaving only smoke visible and spreading downwind toward them.

"Could you tell where it is?" Marianna asked anxiously. The twilight distorted distances, and she could not tell from her brief glimpse how close the flames were to the Girls' Shelter.

Aunt Myriah, who had found opera glasses in her reticule, scanned the smoke intently. "It looks like the shelter is all right for now." She guessed Marianna's question. "But the fire is close. They'll have to evacuate. It appears to have started in Chinatown, and the wind is spreading it this way."

The alarm began again, this time four tolls followed by peal after peal.

"A four-alarmer now and they're calling for all the volunteer companies," Harold interpreted. "Strange the way it's escalating—almost as though someone had set off a chain reaction. More than one poor soul will be cornered in Chinatown tonight."

The sounds of fire wagon bells had begun to echo across the city as volunteer fire companies answered the call. The wind carried the cries of firefighters already on the scene, along with the crackling roar of flames. A staccato of shallow booms sounded like firecrackers, as the windows of wooden buildings loaded with combustibles exploded.

"Oh!" Marianna caught her breath; her hand flew to her throat as the message Mi Ling's family had found in the laundry suddenly became clear. It had not been about dragon fire on a street corner in Chinatown. It had been a message to the Dragon to start a fire on August 30 in Chinatown, and that fire was to corner C.T.—Cole

Taylor. The Dragon had been warned not to slip up this time, as he had on the Fourth of July.

The web of plots and violence was difficult to explain; convincing her skeptical aunt she was not imagining it all was even harder.

"Harold, tell her!" Marianna pleaded, finally. She was running out of time; the fire was spreading.

"I was on board the ship that tried to ram Taylor," Harold admitted flatly. "We were told not to leave any survivors."

Marianna gasped in astonishment; she had known he was involved in piracy, but she had never dreamed he would knowingly participate in murder.

"It was the first and only time I helped with one of Mr. Tremaine's shadier business deals," Harold went on. "Now maybe I'll have a chance to make up for what I tried to do. I'll find Taylor and warn him."

"No!" Aunt Myriah had tears in her eyes, but she was squaring her shoulders, ready for action. "Let Marianna do that. You and I will take care of a more dangerous job. Six girls with babies and two new staff members, just arrived from the East, are at the Shelter. The staff doesn't know the city, and the girls will be too frightened to do anything. We have to get to them."

"Marianna can't travel these streets alone, especially tonight. It isn't safe!"

"No, it's not, but I have a feeling that very soon there may not be any safe place in this city. It will take a man to do what has to be done at the shelter, but without me there, no one will follow your orders. We'll have to trust God to go with Marianna."

"*Vaya con Dios*, go with God." The Spanish people of old California used the phrase for farewell, and newcomers had adopted it unthinkingly as a synonym for "good-by." Tonight Harold murmured the words in Marianna's ear as he enveloped her in a quick hug, and she knew he meant them.

The streets were dark and growing darker. Someone had had the foresight to turn off the gas in the street lamps. All that was needed to spread the fire throughout the city was one explosion; ruptured gas lines would do the rest. Light from the moon and stars was quickly being blotted out as smoke covered the city.

The smells and sounds of the fire intensified as Marianna descended the hillside. She walked rapidly, breaking into a run only when someone tried to speak to her or a crowd of men were gathering on the boardwalk. It was ten blocks at least to the '49ers' fire station. She prayed as she walked that Cole and the engine would still be there or, if they were not, someone could carry her warning to the fire.

On every street merchants and homeowners worked feverishly to douse their buildings with buckets of water. At one intersection a bucket brigade was bringing water from a fountain in the nearby square to pour on the dry wooden planks that surfaced the avenue while frightened horses galloped past them, pulling their carriages, with or without the drivers.

The smoke was thickening, stinging Marianna's eyes and making her choke as she gulped for air. The streets in the direction of the fire disgorged vapors and people into the avenue.

At the corner of one square she was surprised to hear music and laughter coming from a brightly lit building—the Eureka Gambling Palace. She ran past, ignoring the bleary-eyed men who called out to her. As she passed she heard a garbled voice shout, "A thousand dollars says she burns all the way to Sacramento Avenue." Another answered, "Two thousand if it takes out the wharves!"

Betting, in a saloon sitting directly in the path of the flames, on how much of the city would burn! Should she warn them of the direction the winds were blowing? No, they probably knew already and didn't care. Besides, she was not sure she had the courage to face the men who hung out around the open doorway and, if she did, whether they would listen to her.

From the distance came the sounds of fire bells, men's shouts, horses' whinnies, and the roar of wind-whipped flames. An orange-red glow lit the sky over the rooftops.

Marianna could not tell how much was the afterglow of the sunset and how much was the glare from the flames.

The street sign ahead told her she was nearing the '49er fire station, and she began to run. No lights shone in the clubhouse upstairs, but the fire doors were open. Her heart beating rapidly, she ran through the doors and looked eagerly around. The station was empty.

Now what? Cole was gone, and she could see no one to send after him. Should she go to the marshal's office again? The deputy she had talked to before had not been much help. If he had figured out the Dragon's message, he had not managed to do anything about it. She wished Aunt Myriah hadn't taken Harold with her. This, too, seemed to be a man-sized job. If Cole were already at the fire, it would be too late to warn him; she needed a man to stop the Dragon.

"But I don't have a man; there's only me," Marianna said aloud and added the prayer, "Dear Lord, please send me some help. I can't do it alone." She sank onto the floor of the station and rested her head on her arms. Never in her life had she felt so alone.

CHAPTER 16

SOMETHING COLD AND WET touched Marianna's neck. She jumped up—terror-filled images of rats and evil-eyed men racing through her brain—to find two black-and-white spotted Dalmatians studying her curiously. The dogs whined and gave their tails a tentative wag.

Nearly hysterical with relief, Marianna started to laugh. "Lord, I hope this isn't all the help you're sending me!"

But the dogs did give her an idea. She called them to follow her and feeling her way, climbed the fire station's steps to the club room. The drapes had not been drawn across the windows, so she could see well enough to cross the room to the swinging doors. The tip-tapping of the dogs' nails on the hardwood floors gave her confidence to find her way down the dark hall to Cole's office.

"Come on, old dears." She kept up a steady monologue to the dogs. Their little barks and whines in reply gave her a feeling of comradship.

The view from Cole's office window took her breath away. Driven by the wind, flames were racing over rooftops toward the wharves. Out in the bay the waters sent back a yellow-tongued reflection, and billowing smoke rolled toward the west.

Thank God Harold had gone with Aunt Myriah! The Girls' Shelter was near the path of the fire, but after three years Harold knew the city; he would find a way to safety if only he reached the shelter in time. Her heart ached at the thought of the beautiful old ship engulfed in flames, but she shook off the mental picture and closed her eyes to the living picture outside the window. "Help them, Lord" was all the prayer she had time for.

She set about looking through Cole's desk for a scarf or glove—anything that might have his scent. "Back East fire dogs are trained to find people lost in a fire. The firemen just give the dogs something that belonged to the people, and the dogs do the rest," she told the animals. She found a pair of gloves and offered one to each. "I don't know if you are trained that way, but you look intelligent, and I'll bet you want to find Cole as much as I."

The dogs took the gloves gingerly, then dug their noses into the leather, whimpering as they caught the scent.

"Now what we're going to do is go to the fire and find Cole." The words "find Cole" drew an excited bark from the dogs, so she repeated them over and over while feeling her way back down the dark hall, across the recreation room, and down the steps. The dogs, each still holding a glove tightly in its teeth, stayed close at her heels.

Outside, the acrid smell of the fire was closer. The smoke, pushed along by gusts of wind, was darker and thicker. The air was hot and difficult to breathe.

The arrow-straight streets were a double hazard. Their wooden planking—some of it pine and laced with pitch—was fuel for the fire. At the same time, the long, unbending stretches let the flames race forward, unimpeded, like wind down a tunnel.

Yet the straight streets also marked the shortest path to the fire. Avoiding the avenues that showed the heaviest volume of traffic, she turned up a smaller parallel street and began to run.

"Hey, lady! You're going the wrong way. That way's the fire!"

"Come back! Come back!"
"No way out that way."
"You'll be trapped!"

Concerned voices called after her, but she raced on, stopping only long enough to get her breath, then running again toward the noise and the confusion of the fire.

A fire engine, its team of horses plunging fearfully, its round bulk covered with clinging volunteer fighters, rattled past her on its way to the fire. Another, blackened with smoke, raced in the opposite direction, and Marianna guessed it had run out of water and was hurrying to replenish its supply. She doubted it would return in time. The fire was spreading rapidly; the orange-yellow glare ahead stretched nearly from one end of the horizon to the other.

The dogs stayed close beside her. Occasionally they glanced back over their shoulders and whined, as if to suggest she change directions, but they did not turn back, and when she ran, they bounded ahead of her.

More than once Marianna wished she had looked for a gun or some other weapon in Cole's office. A sailor, too drunk to understand the danger, grabbed at her from a dark alley. Rough men jostled against her, and once a pair of respectable-looking citizens seized her arms and tried to drag her back down the street to safety. Each time the dogs came to her rescue, baring their teeth and lunging at the men's throats until the men broke away, yelling to others along the way about the crazy lady and her mad dogs.

"Perhaps the Lord knew the best kind of help after all," Marianna talked aloud to herself. One man could not have protected her nearly so well as this pair of dogs. Moreover, a man would probably have wasted precious time trying to argue her out of going. A picture of Cole Taylor's fury if he knew what she was doing flashed across her mind. She could almost hear him yelling at her, "Marianna, how could you do something so stupid?"

How? It was easy if you loved someone and you were convinced he was in danger.

The air crackled with sparks as she approached the fire line. Marianna remembered her straw bonnet, pulled it off, and wrapped her handkerchief around her curls. She doused herself and the dogs thoroughly with water from a watering trough beside the street. A wrap more sturdy than her three-tiered cape would have been preferable, but soaked in water and tied with its sopping wool lining on the outside, it should offer some protection. She took the gloves from the dogs and put them on, hardly noticing how her hands swam in them and how she had to double her fists to keep them on.

She had finished her preparations and was calling the dogs to follow when a frantic braying nearby stopped her. A vendor's donkey had run away with its cart. The cart had overturned, spilling its load of apples and oranges over the street and trapping the animal.

Marianna hesitated only a moment. Ignoring the pains searing through her lungs, she ran toward the donkey.

"Be quiet now!" she shouted at the dogs to hush their barking.

The donkey put his ears back and began kicking at the downed cart with swift double jabs of his back hoofs. With those hoofs so busy, she could not get close enough to unhitch the cart, so instead she tried to heave it upright. The cart wouldn't budge. She pulled at it, pushed it, turned her back and heaved with her legs. She had started looking around for something to use as a lever when two men ran out of the smoke.

"We'll help you with that, ma'am." They grabbed the cart on the down side, gave a mighty shove, and while it rocked into place, ran back into the darkness.

"Thank you, Lord," Marianna murmured, then cautiously approached the donkey's head. She half expected him to bolt, but he stood with his ears back and one nervous eye following her. She spoke soothingly. "Everything's fine now, but I think you had better come with us. Besides, we might need you. If things get too bad, I'll unhitch your cart and ride you out of here straight to the top of Telegraph Hill." She looked somewhat dubiously at the animal's swaying back and jumpy hindquarters, but if the worst came she could at least try it.

She was at the edge of Chinatown now and so near the blaze her skin burned with the heat. The atmosphere was ominous. A few die-hards were removing possessions from their stores and homes, and looters were hauling off the contents of a display through a broken store window. But most streets were deserted. The rows of shops with the brightly painted signs of dragons and pagodas looked luridly threatening in the glare from the fire.

Marianna half expected to see a dragon—this time alive and breathing real fire—round the corner and weave toward her on its long serpent's tail.

"God goes with me. I'm not afraid," she repeated over and over, first to herself and then aloud to the donkey, snorting with fear and the dogs whose tails were tucked between their legs and whose constant whimpers showed even their stout courage was failing.

If the streets nearby were like ovens, the fire line itself was an inferno. The glare was blinding. A row of buildings, three and four stories high, was engulfed in flames. Fire, leaping twenty or thirty feet into the air, licked angrily at the sky. Black smoke surged skyward, then fell back on blasts of wind that brought down showers of sparks and burning debris.

Ranged bravely in front of the fire were the firefighters and their engines. Long streams of water spouted into the air and fell, seemingly without effect, into the heart of the flames. Silhouetted against the blaze, the men looked tiny and helpless but valiant beyond Marianna's imagination.

The noise was deafening. The shouts of men giving and answering orders were barely discernible amid the roar of flames and the screams of terrified horses, unhitched from the fire engines but held in readiness close by.

Marianna watched spellbound. The glare and smoke burned her eyes; her skin reddened with the heat and mottled under the sharp sting of flying sparks. Every breath hurt.

Then a window above her head exploded, sending shards of glass crashing into the street. A painted paper dragon perched atop the building caught fire and began to writhe on its board frame.

Grabbing the donkey's halter and calling the dogs, Marianna ran toward an alley. The tears streaming down her face obscured her vision; she stumbled and fell but held onto the reins. As she scrambled to her feet she caught a motion at the edge of her vision and whirled just in time to see a burly shape emerge from behind a building. She must have screamed because the man turned toward her; the familiar hook nose and jutting jaw were outlined clearly in the firelight. It was the Dragon. An evil grin spread over his face, and he started forward, only to fall back as the Dalmatians leaped at him, growling and snapping.

"I will trust and not be afraid." "No weapon formed against thee shall prosper." "A thousand shall fall at thy side, and ten thousand at thy right hand, but it shall not come nigh thee." "Fear thou not; for I am with thee." The Scriptures winged their way into Marianna's consciousness from somewhere deep inside.

The Dragon stopped, shook his fist at her, and with a scowl of hate, ran off into the night.

"Thank you again, Lord," she remembered to say before she called back the dogs and, holding the gloves, reminded them, "Find Cole. Find Cole."

They sniffed the gloves, cried and ran in circles, but wouldn't leave her.

"Please, please try," she begged them, this time giving them a little push. Still nothing.

"I guess we'll have to go together."

The upper floor of the building was burning. The fire sprayed the alley behind it with glowing cinders, but its light did not reach into the shadows.

"Find Cole," Marianna kept repeating while the dogs pressed, whining, against her skirts and the donkey pulled on its halter, resisting going under the burning missiles. It took a few minutes to adjust her eyes from the blinding light of the fire. Spots swam across her vision—purple, gray, and yellow. The yellow spot, not glowing and bright like a spark but soft and muted like a splash of colored cloth, drew her eyes back again.

Giving the donkey's head a yank, she inched into the

alley until her foot nudged something black and splashed with yellow.

Cole's hat—the one that had been ruined by yellow paint. He must have grabbed it when he answered the fire alarm, thinking it was already too damaged to save.

"He must be somewhere close by," she told the dogs. "Find him! Find Cole."

This time they went bounding from shadow to shadow, snuffing at dark shapes and pushing their noses into cracks and doorways. One dog disappeared into a sunken stairwell, then leaped out again as a flaming timber crashed down from the roof. The other jumped a low fence and began to bark.

Her heart pounding, Marianna ran, dragging the donkey with her toward the barking. What she saw brought fresh tears to her eyes, and she dropped to her knees beside Cole's still body.

He was sprawled on his back in an irrigation ditch. The mud oozed around him, smearing his hands and coating his clothes. For a moment she was afraid to touch him; then her hand placed gingerly on his chest found it rising and falling in shallow breaths, and she began quickly to examine his shoulders and arms for injuries. She half expected a bullet wound, but she found only a sticky wetness, warmer than the irrigation mud, on the side of his head.

"Cole, wake up. It's Marianna. Please, wake up."

She tried to rouse him, but her calls and nudges only brought a low moan. She had no time to go for help. Above their heads another rooftop was catching fire. The donkey pranced nervously, but he didn't break away from the fence where Marianna had tied him.

"We're going to have to get him into the cart," she told the dogs. But how? He was twice her size. "When you have a heavy patient, don't lift; drag him," she remembered her sister the nurse saying.

Whipping off her cape, she laid it on the ground, then slowly rolled Cole until he was half in and half out of the ditch and lying on her cape. She had to take off his gloves to get a firm grip on the cape's edge. Bracing her heels in the dirt, she pulled and pulled until he was out of the ditch and sliding over the ground.

Getting him over the fence was a problem. The poles were firmly set in the earth. The top rail was only three feet from the ground, but she could not lift a heavy man even that high. A nudge of her foot, however, showed the bottom rail was loose. She kicked it free, stubbing her toes in the process. Cole barely fit beneath the rail, and he moaned softly as she dragged him under.

The alley was getting hotter and brighter. The air danced with flying cinders as the fire crept down from the roofs of the buildings, running along the wooden edges and ringing the window sills. Glass, heated and pressured from inside, burst along the upper floors. The fire hissed and growled as it stretched in flaming arcs from building to building overhead.

At a loading dock nearby, Marianna found a short ramp. Positioning it from the ground into the donkey cart took precious minutes; the animal shifted forward and back nervously, his eyes glazing with fear. Finally, Marianna took the kerchief off her head and tied it securely around the donkey's eyes. His ears continued to twitch, but he stood still while she tugged and pulled the unconscious man up the ramp and into the cart.

She had hoped to drive the cart and make better speed. Now, with the donkey's eyes covered, she had to lead him at a walk from the burning alley.

Only minutes had passed, though they had seemed like hours; yet in that short time the fire line had shifted. The engines she had expected to see no more than a half block away had moved down another street. Even while Marianna watched, a building began to crumble. Tumbling like a fiery waterfall, it blocked the street with burning debris. On the other side she could still see the firefighters and their futile streams of water, but they were cut off.

Bewildered, she looked around her. Surely God had not brought her this far to fail her now! Behind the cart, where the alley had been, was a wall of flames. To the right, sloping down toward the bay, was a blazing avenue of board planks. To the left she turned and felt, rather than saw, the difference. Burning buildings were on each side of the street, but between them was a narrow path and beyond, darkness all the way to the top of Telegraph Hill.

"He'll always make a way of escape," Marianna said thankfully as she led the donkey and followed the dogs toward the opening. Upwind of the fire the air was cooler, touched with a salty sea dampness that mingled ocean smells with the acrid stink of the fire. Afraid to stop in case the wind shifted, Marianna hurried along a broad street that cut across the base of the hill. The eerie feeling of being alone on a flaming earth was dissipating as she saw other refugees like herself, carrying belongings or helping the injured. They called out bits of news to each other.

"Montgomery is blocked."

"Kearny Street's in flames."

"They're dynamiting warehouses along the docks."

The dogs were whimpering. Their coats were singed; the pads of their feet, burned. The donkey was breathing heavily.

An old woman with a tiny baby strapped to her back had stopped to rest beside a watering trough.

"Can you tell me how to get to the top of Telegraph Hill?" Marianna asked.

The woman pointed to a steep flight of steps behind her.

"But isn't there a street? I can't take this cart up a stairway. I have a wounded man inside."

The woman looked curiously in the cart, but she would or could say nothing about a street. Her eyes had a glazed expression as though some shock or tragedy had left her dazed, her body still functioning but not her mind.

Water remained in the trough, tepid and smelling of horses, but it felt wonderful on Marianna's parched lips and throat. She untied her handkerchief from around the donkey's eyes and dipped it in the water to wash Cole's face and moisten his lips. His mud-streaked face terrified her. She could not tell how much of the mess caking the side of his head was blood; to her heightened imagination, the entire side of his head seemed a pulpy mass.

Still, his heart was beating; his breathing seemed stronger in the cooler air; and his moans were less frequent. He even opened his mouth long enough for her to squeeze into it some water from a wet rag.

Impulsively Marianna reached down and pressed her lips gently to his. "Please don't die," she whispered. "I love you."

Cautiously, the donkey drank a few mouthfuls, then felt his way along the trough, looking for the clearest, tastiest pools. The dogs, on the other hand, leaped in with all four feet and lapped eagerly.

Refreshed and feeling more hopeful, Marianna tried to get her bearings. The area under Telegraph Hill was the site of the worst slums in the city, with no street lights or boardwalks. The houses were little more than shacks; the streets, dirt.

This is one time conveniences are not advantages, Marianna thought, recalling the flaming planked roads and dangerous gas lines of uptown.

She finally found a dirt street that was more path than road, but it seemed to lead upward.

Slowly, they climbed, stopping every few minutes to rest the donkey. Marianna resisted the temptation to look behind and kept her eyes firmly on the hilltop. Far away she heard an explosion—probably the warehouses along the shoreline or blocks of buildings elsewhere being dynamited to make fire lanes. The bells had stopped tolling, perhaps because every volunteer in the city plus many others were already on the job. From somewhere out in the harbor came the sharp blasts of a steamship whistle, alternating long and short notes in what sounded like a message code.

For the first time in hours, Marianna wondered what had happened to Harold and Aunt Myriah. Had they made it safely to the shelter? Had they rescued the girls and their babies? Were they all together now on that steamship, safe across the waters of the bay?

Mi Ling would be safe on her husband's truck farm far down the peninsula. She breathed a prayer of thanks for that and a prayer of petition for all those in the city behind her who were not safe tonight!

Throngs of people crowded together at the top of Telegraph Hill. A white hospital tent with a giant red cross had been set up near the summit. At other tents people lay on blankets or drank steaming cups of coffee and tea.

As she turned around, Marianna unconsciously closed her eyes, then opened them and stared, her heart pounding. All of Chinatown was burning. The fire stretched south and west along avenues of flame, and out over the bay the wooden wharves flared orange-red above the water. At the edge of the harbor, some ships, too slow to put to sea, were afire. The flames died down and leaped up in an eerie pulsing rhythm as explosions ripped through blocks or buildings collapsed. And over it all rose clouds of thick, ugly smoke that shut out the heavens.

CHAPTER 17

A SALTY BREEZE SWEPT IN from the ocean, scattering the thin fog and bringing flights of gulls wheeling across the morning sun. From the top of Telegraph Hill semaphore messages flashed to ships standing in the bay. A narrow line of sailing vessels moved on the morning tide toward the Golden Gate, just visible through white fog curtains.

How wonderful it was to greet the dawn alive! "Weeping may endure for a night, but joy cometh in the morning." From the crest of the hill Marianna watched the pink and salmon lights in the east change to a golden glow and knew what it was to be truly thankful for a new day.

Below a few fires still burned in the city, but for the most part blackened ruins with only an occasional flicker of flame lay where Chinatown had been. Charred gashes reached along the avenues and spread out over the waterfront. The neighborhood of beached ships near the old harbor was gone; from a distance not a single mast or deck was visible; the weathered docks, the old ships, the shops, the Girls' Shelter had been swept away by the fire or perhaps blasted by the fire crews.

Surprisingly, much of the city had survived. To the south toward the peninsula, Marianna could see broad avenues and wide squares untouched by the disaster. Little traffic was moving, yet San Francisco was not asleep. Clusters of people stood in the streets and on the hills, surveying the damage as she was and trying to decide where to begin to clean up the mess and start again.

Somewhere in the crowd around her a lone quavery voice began to sing shakily:

> *Amazing grace, how sweet the sound,*
> *That saved a wretch like me.*
> *I once was lost, but now I'm found.*
> *'Twas blind, but now I see.*

Other voices, cracked and rough from hours of breathing smoke and fumes, joined in.

> *Thro' many dangers toils and snares,*
> *I have already come;*
> *'Tis grace that brought me safe thus far,*
> *And grace will lead me home.*

Tears were in the eyes and on the cheeks of burly men and hard-faced women when the singers had finished. *This is one disaster from which the Lord is already bringing good,* Marianna thought, and she wiped the moisture from her own eyelashes. Many of these people had had narrow escapes they would not soon forget. *Washington may still be far away, but God and heaven are not. They know that now.*

Lost in her musings, she almost did not feel the tug at her skirt and hear an insistent voice repeating, "Miss, Miss, you said to call you when Mr. Taylor woke up."

"What?" Marianna looked down at the face of the child without recognition for a moment. Then she remembered this was the daughter of the woman who had offered to sit with Cole. After a sleepless night of bathing his face and watching him toss and turn on a bed of gunnysacks and army blankets, she was too tired to think straight.

"Miss, aren't you listening? You said to tell you about Mr. Taylor."

A sudden stab of fear constricted Marianna's throat. "He's not . . ."

"It's nothing to make you go all white like that." The child's voice was plaintive now, almost a whine. "He just woke up; that's all. And you're supposed to come so my ma and I can go back home."

Cole was in a corner of the big hospital tent, his makeshift bed against a canvas wall that moved slowly, making a sound that was a cross between the crack of a whip and the thud of a carpet beater. The right side of his head was covered with a large bandage. The blow to his head—probably made by a large club or stick, the doctor had said—had been his only injury. With the mud cleaned away and color returning to his face, he was no longer a sight to inspire terror.

His head, elevated by a grain-sack pillow, was facing away from her as Marianna approached, but the pleasantly round woman who sat beside him rose, gathered her knitting in a bag, and slipped smilingly away. The two Dalmatians, who lay one on each side of Cole, thumped their tails in welcome.

"Christina, how did you ever find me?"

Marianna's heart, which had been soaring, plunged abruptly back to earth. "The least you could do after I went to all the trouble of pulling you out of that inferno last night is get my name right!"

"Marianna!" The shout brought a chorus of "Quiet!" "Shush!" "Keep it down!" from across the hospital tent. Cole reached for her and pulled her down beside him, wincing as the action jarred his head again. "What do you mean you pulled me out of an inferno? The woman who was here just said a pretty girl, a friend of mine, had sat with me all night."

"And you assumed that pretty girl had to be Christina." Marianna glanced down at her dress—the same green yoke-necked merino gown she had put on to wear aboard the *Atlantis* yesterday but now streaked with soot, torn at the hem and shoulders, and marked with dozens of tiny holes where sparks and cinders had struck her. She had washed her face and felt the tiny burns on her cheeks and chin; she could only imagine what her hair looked like, tumbling around her face, frizzed and broken in places where it had been singed. At least her eyelashes and brows had not been burned off like those of some people she had seen that morning. Still she doubted she looked pretty at all, in spite of what the woman who sat with Cole had said, and suddenly being pretty mattered very, very much to Marianna.

"You haven't answered me," Cole was insisting. "We're on Telegraph Hill, aren't we? How did I get here? Where did you come from? Where are Harold and your aunt? Why are the dogs from the firehouse here?"

Taking a deep breath, Marianna launched into the explanation, sticking to bare facts, adding details only when he questioned her, but she could tell from the way his face turned white that the story was graphic enough as it stood.

It did not help when a fellow '49er from Cole's club found them and supplied more descriptions. "We caught the Dragon last night. He boasted that he had left you and some girl in the heart of the fire—the part they're calling Hell's Kitchen. But we couldn't get back to you." The man's voice shook with emotion. Cole's shook with anger.

"You had no business coming after me. You could have been killed."

"And where would you be if I hadn't come? I had to do something. That deputy marshal hadn't helped at all." Then she had another explanation to make. This time Cole flushed red and looked embarrassed.

"He warned me, thought I might be the C.T. in the note," he admitted. "I didn't take it seriously." He lay back and closed his eyes for a minute. The bandage gave him a rakish look, and Marianna resisted an impulse to smooth back the curl that had fallen over his forehead.

"Why did you do it?"

"I had to," she answered bravely, with just a hint of laughter. "I owed it to my twelve children."

Cole's eyes snapped open. "What twelve children?"

"The ones I plan to have. Don't you remember? You

said Harold wouldn't be up to having so many, but I thought you might be, and I couldn't take a chance on something happening to my children's father." The words came out in a rush, and Marianna blushed at her daring. That was giving him honesty with a vengeance!

Cole, however, laughed delightedly. "I can see why you would want to hold onto me then. Must not be many men around who could handle such an ambitious plan." He began to pull her down to him, then noticed the hand resting on his chest and nearly shouted in exasperation, "Marianna, will you please take that ring off your finger!"

The pearl engagement ring, forgotten even when Marianna had told Harold she couldn't marry him—had that been only two nights before?—still circled her finger, but something had happened to the pearl. Seared by the heat of the fires, perhaps grazed by a burning ember that had left a long welt across her hand, it had shriveled. The once satiny surface was brown and flaking like the crumbled petal of a withered rose.

"Poor thing. I'll miss it," Marianna sighed wistfully, all the while watching Cole from beneath lowered lashes. "After all, I wore it for years."

Cole scowled and pulled her possessively into his arms. "I'll replace it with a sapphire to match your eyes, or at least I will if the fire hasn't ruined me."

A sapphire. Just what Marianna had always wanted, and she hadn't even given him a hint. "I think we were made for each other. I love you so much," she whispered before she returned his kiss.

The cheer that went up around the hospital tent reminded them they were not alone. Marianna, her face rosier than ever, pulled her arms from around his neck, but Cole released her reluctantly, the teasing grin she loved spreading over his face.

"Now you'll have to marry me," he said in a voice loud enough for everyone to hear. "I have witnesses."

A chorus of voices spoke up in agreement.

"We heard all right."

"Can't get out of it now."

"California has laws against breach of promise."

"I'll give the bride away."

In spite of his new-found happiness, Cole was a less-than-satisfactory patient. The doctor refused to let him get up, claiming twenty-four hours of complete rest was necessary after a blow to the head.

"But I have a business to look after, property to check over, damages to assess."

"I cannot be responsible for the consequences if you won't follow my advice," the doctor had argued. "You could cause yourself permanent injury."

"I'll take the responsibility," Cole was saying when Marianna pointed out that he had nothing on under the blankets except a nightshirt.

"And you don't get your pants or your shoes until the doctor says so."

Cole looked startled; then he grinned. "Just what I needed. A woman who always has to have the last word."

It was nearly noon before Aunt Myriah and Harold found their way to Telegraph Hill. They and all the people from the shelter had spent the night on a steamship out in the bay.

"I wanted to go back to find you, but we were cut off," Harold explained.

"No need for apologies," Aunt Myriah cut in brusquely, though she looked as relieved as her stepson to find her niece unharmed. "Marianna was supposed to have gone to a fire station, not the fire."

They had news about acquaintances, about the cleanup and rebuilding already underway in the city, and even about Cole's property.

"One of your warehouses had to be dynamited," Harold told Cole, "but the rest are unharmed."

"Looks like you get your sapphire after all." Cole winked at Marianna.

Aunt Myriah bristled a little at that. "Correct me if I'm wrong, but I was under the impression my niece is still engaged to my stepson. If that is the case, she will not be accepting any sapphires from you, young man."

"Let it go, Mother." Harold hushed the old lady before Cole or Marianna had a chance to say anything. "Marianna and I came to an understanding some time ago. From now on we're cousins and good friends."

He turned to Cole and held out a hand. "Does that sound all right to you?"

If Cole still felt any jealousy for his former rival, it was not apparent as they shook hands. Marianna's quick eye caught a flash of gold passing from hand to hand and realized Cole had returned her engagement ring.

"A sapphire will suit her better anyway," Harold said gruffly and pocketed the shattered pearl. "With your permission, though, I'd like to have the pearl replaced and give it back to her as a keepsake, this time from a cousin who will always care about her."

Cole nodded, but Marianna made up her mind never to put that ring back on her finger. Perhaps someday she would have a daughter who could wear it.

Aunt Myriah, who had listened without interruption since her stepson had taken control of the conversation, now let out a sound that was half snort and half sigh. "Well, I can't say I didn't see this coming. I always counted on Marianna's being the daughter I never had, but I guess I can settle for her being a favorite niece.

"Now, though, we have a problem. I am scheduled to leave for home immediately, and my niece cannot possibly stay here by herself. I'm sure you both had hopes for a September wedding, but I think you had better revise your plans and make it next spring in Philadelphia."

To Marianna's amazement, Cole agreed. "After all, I need to speak with your father or some other male relative. With all due respect to Harold, it wouldn't be right for me to ask him for your hand."

Then she remembered her brother-in-law's letter. "We already have the permission of a male member of my family. My brother-in-law approves of you. He wrote to tell me so."

Later, when Harold and Aunt Myriah had gone to find a place to spend the night, she explained the contents of that letter—the identity of John Tilton, the suspicions that had clouded her judgment, the coincidences that had undermined her trust.

"I thought about never telling you, but I didn't want any secrets between us. Can you ever forgive me?"

He could, but his forgiveness carried a price tag. "Shall we say one kiss for every suspicious thought you had about me?"

Since Marianna had had many suspicious thoughts and their kisses tended to be somewhat lengthy, paying that bill promised to take a very long time.

"I'm not going home, you know," she told him finally.

"I hate to see you go, but I agree with your aunt. I don't see any other way."

"I told you once that in the unlikely event we should get married, I was not going to stay waiting meekly at home while you traveled? Well, that applies also to going meekly back to Philadelphia to wait for you. Cole, you have tried to send me home twice, and I haven't gone. Do you really believe I would go now? Besides, what kind of Christian would I be if I left now when I am most needed?"

CHAPTER 18

THE NEEDS WERE GREATEST in the days immediately following the fire. With Chinatown and the waterfront little more than rubble, a third of San Francisco's poorest inhabitants were without food or shelter. They could not even camp among the ruins, for the authorities had ordered the area evacuated while burned-out buildings were dynamited and the debris hauled away.

The temporary camp on Telegraph Hill became semi-permanent, and tent cities once again fringed the metropolis.

"Reminds me of '49," Cole told Marianna, and she thought, *Someday I'll be able to look back and say, "This reminds me of the big fire in '55."* It felt good to be part of the history and the birth of the city. Soon she would be calling herself an "Old" San Franciscan.

She did not leave with Aunt Myriah and Harold. They sailed on the *Atlantis* when the ship put out to sea forty-eight hours later with a full load of refugees and news for the Eastern papers.

"This is one part of the family that probably shouldn't be at the wedding anyway." The old lady had finally agreed to leaving her. "No girl needs long faces around when she gets married or any reminders either. Don't know what I'm going to tell my brother, though."

Before she said good-by, she gave Marianna her pearls. "Always intended them for you anyway, but it would have made things easier if you had married Harold. Now I suppose I'll have to come up with something for your sisters, Gloriana and Juliana, just to keep things fair."

Aunt Myriah was right. Hers and Harold's presence at the wedding would have brought regret into a day of joy. Still, it made Marianna's heart ache to think of spending that most important day of her life without any members of her family close by.

Cole was sympathetic, but he was too involved in mopping up the damages to worry about their wedding. When she insisted on staying, she had imagined a hurry-up affair, perhaps in a week's time, with Christina Dowling as her matron of honor. *We can wear party dresses anyway,* she had thought, finding the prospect rather flat after her vision of a lace gown sewn with rows and rows of tiny seed pearls, but anything elaborate would have seemed inappropriate when San Francisco mourned its losses and thousands were homeless.

Cole, however, seemed to be in no hurry. He had placed Marianna under Christina's care and gone about his work, ignoring both the doctor's and his fiancée's pleas that he "take it easy" while his head wound healed.

"I had a much worse bash in the head on the Sacramento River," was his answer. "It was back in '50 when someone tried to jump my gold claim."

Marianna and Christina were busy too. As secretary and chairperson for the Chinatown Girls' Shelter Foundation, they were faced with hundreds of appeals at a time when their shelter and supplies had been lost and they could find little to spare anywhere in San Francisco. While they searched once again for a facility, they set up temporary operations in an abandoned storefront owned by Cole. They still looked longingly at the huge multi-storied house Jacques Tremaine had owned.

Tremaine himself was gone. He had not been seen since the fire, and rumors were that he had ordered the fire's start and had paid for his treachery by being caught in it. Marianna subscribed to another theory. Tremaine's empire had been destroyed by the fire. He would have no reason to stay in San Francisco and, if he were Gloriana's John Tilton, every reason to leave, with an army investigator on his trail. Marianna remembered the deed to a Black Hills gold mine and felt sorry for the inhabitants. At least there Tremaine or Tilton or whatever his name was would not find any more Windemere sisters to threaten.

But with Tremaine gone, the Gingerbread House, as Marianna had come to call it, had somehow acquired a new owner. Almost daily on her way to the temporary shelter, Marianna saw broken glass being replaced in the windows, shaped shingles repaired in the siding, and fresh coats of paint applied to every sculptured eave, decorated gable, and ornate border of swirled and carved trim.

"Someone truly loves the place to spend so much fixing it up right now when a nail is worth a gold nugget in San Francisco." She consoled herself with that knowledge but could not escape a certain wistful homesickness whenever she saw the place.

Cole did remember her ring. Calling for her in his one-horse buggy, he took her to dinner at the hotel on Portsmouth Square, where she had first stayed with her aunt. The fires had not reached this far, and the gas-lit streets showed no evidence of the recent tragedy.

Marianna had put on the same rose silk that had seemed almost dowdy her first evening in San Francisco, but tonight with her aunt's double string of pearls clasped around her neck and Cole looking at her adoringly, she felt elegant. She had briefly considered wearing the matching pearl ring, which Harold had somehow replaced before he left, then remembered her resolution and left it behind. That ring had stood between her and Cole for too long, and she needed no reminders of their estrangement tonight.

"Not sorry you stayed, are you?" The anxious expression in his eyes told Marianna tonight was the time to create glorious new memories, not to relive bittersweet old ones.

How eager he was to please her! Their table was in a secluded corner where the glitter and glare of the hotel's enormous chandeliers were muted enough to allow the soft glow of candlelight. Gold- and pink-tinged rosebuds stood in a crystal vase on the table. There were cool goblets of a delicately yellow fruit that Cole called pineapple "from the Sandwich Islands, thousands of miles to the west."

Dinner consisted of course after course of delicacies, designed to tempt a woman's appetite rather than satisfy a man's—more of the pineapple, this time in large luscious chunks in a fruit salad with delicate pink melon balls, rosy watermelon, and golden slices of orange; cracked crab to be lifted from the shell with tiny silver forks and dipped in spicy melted butter; asparagus tips in a creamy Hollandaise sauce; filets of poached salmon garnished with lemon wedges; and slabs of broiled morel mushrooms. Dessert was a Black Forest cake, so tall and light it folded over the fork, served with steaming cups of a spiced tea that tasted of cloves and oranges and smelled of orange blossoms.

While they ate, they talked or sat in a companionable silence of gentle looks and smiles. Several times Marianna saw Cole reach into his vest pocket only to pause and pull his fingers out again as though he were waiting for the perfect moment.

He is doing everything he can to make this evening magic for me, Marianna realized, and she vowed to herself that she would never let him know how lonely and lost she felt at the thought of being married so far from home and family.

When she could not eat another bite, Cole suggested they walk on the veranda. The evening air was cool with a hint of fog like a tracery of spiderwebs veiling the moon and stars. Cole tucked her shawl around her shoulders and left his arm there.

"Did I tell you how beautiful you are this evening?"

"Several times," she laughed to disguise the little

catch in her breath and wondered if she would ever be able to feel the touch of this man's hand or hear the teasing caress in his voice without her heart's skipping a beat.

"Then did I tell you how much I love you and how much I thank God for bringing you into my life?"

"Yes, but please tell me again."

Instead, he showed her with a kiss that was gentleness itself, followed by another so ardent she pulled away, breathless and laughing.

Then he took the ring from his pocket and slipped it on her finger. An enormous marquise-cut sapphire was set in a constellation of yellow diamond baguettes, and all around the gems was a delicate filigree of beaten gold.

"The nuggets from my first and only gold strike." He showed her a matching band of gold and smiled teasingly. "You get the rest of my gold-rush fortune when I return from the north next month and you meet me at the altar to say 'I do.' "

That month passed slowly. During the mornings, Marianna worked at the shelter teaching housekeeping, cooking, and plain sewing; fancy needlework, they had decided, could wait until the basic needs were taken care of. In the afternoon, she helped her hostess with a new project, an orphanage for children left alone by the recent disaster. This work demanded even more of the widow's time and resources than her first venture. To house and support the children, she purchased a hacienda ten miles south of the city. Often Marianna wondered if even Christina's fortune could stand the inroads she was making on it, but she could not deny that the country air and caring for a barnyard filled with animals were dimming the terror in the children's eyes and filling out the poverty-pinched contours of their bodies and faces.

Moreover, traveling to the hacienda gave Marianna a chance to visit her first San Francisco friend, Mi Ling. The former maid was now a grand lady, mistress of a family of young relatives and devoted daughter to an elderly couple who admired everything she did.

"Not all come to Christ yet," she told Marianna, "but all will."

During the little time they were not working, Marianna and Christina planned the wedding. The ceremony was to be held in the beautiful church where they worshiped each week, with the young minister Marianna remembered best for his Jonah-in-the-belly-of-the-whale sermon. A reception at the Dowling estate would follow, and Christina had planned a menu so lavish that Marianna protested.

"You'll have enough to feed an army."

"Haven't you seen the guest list?" Christina countered and reminded her that between the friends Marianna had made in her few months in San Francisco and the crowds of Cole's friends, club members, and employees, at least eight hundred had been invited.

Christina entered fully into the preparations, but whenever Marianna mentioned her being matron of honor, she sidestepped. "I'm not sure I'm ready to let go of my mourning," she said one time, "and you can't have a blackbird next to the bridal dove." Another time she was worried because she usually cried at weddings—"not dainty tears but great gulping sobs"—and she didn't want people to think she didn't approve of the marriage.

Feeling a little bit hurt, Marianna refused Christina's offer to purchase her a gown. "My white muslin with a fresh overdress and matching veil of gauze will be fine," she insisted. The costume was charming if not quite in the fairy-princess style she had always dreamed of. What did it matter if the material was a shade too white to match her precious pearls or no lace was to be had at any price in San Francisco to edge the high neckline and long sleeves?

Besides, with the wedding just days away, she had more important things to worry about.

"If Cole said he wanted to be married in exactly one month, he meant exactly one month," Christina had insisted when the printer asked for the date for the wedding invitations.

Marianna had no doubt she was right, but as the day drew closer, her imagination plagued her with pictures of sunken ships, Indian raids, holdups, and wild animals—all the dangers that typified to her the northern wilderness. When the day of the rehearsal had come and gone and Cole had missed it, she began to consider going after him.

"Lord, you helped me find him once before. I know you can do it again."

Therefore, she was not at all prepared to open the door of her workroom at the shelter and find Cole standing there next to a red-haired giant.

"Did you think I had gotten lost?" Cole asked after he had hugged and kissed her thoroughly, much to the delight of his hulking companion.

"The Windemere sisters just seem to be naturally kissable," the man observed with a grin that made Marianna stare wide-eyed at him. "Now don't disappoint me, little sister. I bet Gloriana the new colt I've been wanting against a sewing machine she has her eye on that you would know me right off."

"Graham!" Marianna squealed and gave her brother-in-law a hug; then before she could catch her breath, Gloriana ran through the door, laughing and scolding her husband.

"Now that doesn't count, Graham. You gave her too big a hint."

The sisters threw their arms around each other, their laughter mingling with tears that did not lessen the joy of that moment in the least. Gloriana's head, topped by a crown of dark curls, reached a full three inches above Marianna's. Her eyes were gray rather than blue, and hours in the sun had warmed her skin to the color of honey. But the long thick eyelashes, the full red lips, the musical voices were the same.

"I think we did very well for ourselves by marrying the Windemere sisters, even if it took some claim jumping on my part," Cole congratulated Graham and himself.

"They tell me Juliana is the pretty one," Graham confided with a teasing grin at his wife.

"Really?" Cole asked innocently. "Do you think I should wait and try my luck with her before it's too late or keep the one I've got?"

"It's already too late, my soon-to-be brother-in-law," Gloriana scolded playfully. "Now if you two men will just go away, we can get down to business."

The business Gloriana had in mind was altering a magnificent wedding gown—all lace and silk and pearls—to Marianna's smaller size.

"I didn't think you would have time to make something," she explained, "so I brought you mine."

The gown was everything Marianna had dreamed of. A half skirt of lace covered yards and yards of silk. Tight lacy sleeves were set in with puffs, and the fitted bodice and dropped waist were covered with seed pearls.

"We'll add a hooped petticoat and leave more neck bare to show off your pearls," Glorianna decided. "Then the only thing you will need is a veil."

The gauze Marianna had planned to wear was tried and discarded. "Too white," the sisters agreed. The gown was a creamy shade that exactly matched Marianna's pearls.

"What you need is lace," Christina, called in for advice on the eve of the wedding, informed them with a mysterious grin. "Wait a minute." She ran out to return a minute later with a lace mantilla of exquisite fineness.

"I had gotten this for you before you refused to let me buy your gown," Christina said as she arranged the lace to fall from a tall comb across Marianna's face and around her shoulders.

"Do you see now why I couldn't be your matron of honor and forgive me?"

They actually are like brother and sister, she realized.

With a brother-in-law to give her away and a sister to stand up with her at the wedding, Marianna's joy was complete.

She was radiant as she followed Gloriana down the aisle of the church, her fingers trembling on Graham's arm but her eyes fixed steadily on Cole. She was vaguely aware of handing her bouquet of pale ivory roses, baby's breath, and maidenhair fern to her sister before stepping to Cole's side at the altar.

"I, Cole, take thee, Marianna, to be my lawfully wedded wife."

"I, Marianna, take thee, Cole, to be my lawfully wedded husband."

"I now pronounce you man and wife. You may kiss the bride."

Cole's fingers fumbled with the delicate lace. He lifted it and folded it back in a white halo, then bent slowly to her lips in a kiss that promised a lifetime of love and caring.

After hours of accepting congratulations and opening gifts, she had fallen asleep leaning against his shoulder in the buggy.

"Marianna, we're home." Cole's whisper brought her eyes fluttering open, but when she looked up at her Gingerbread House, ghostly in the moonlight, she thought she was still dreaming.

"Home?"

"This is the place you wanted, isn't it? I'd hate to think I'd picked the wrong house to raise our twelve children in." He guided her proudly through a scalloped picket fence and up a pathway planted with blossoming fuchsias.

At the doorway he paused a moment. "Happy?" he asked, searching her face with the anxious, eager-to-please look that so delighted her.

"Ecstatically," she told him and, to prove it, clasped her arms daringly around his neck while he swung her off her feet.

Over his shoulder she caught a glimpse of the Golden Gate to San Francisco Bay bathed in the moonlight. Through the gate, catching the late tide, a tall ship moved majestically out to sea. Its sails were filled with the wind and shone like polished silver.

Pressing a kiss on Cole's cheek, Marianna laughed happily and breathed a soft prayer. *Thank you, Lord, for all the golden gates in my life and for the tides and winds to take me through them.*

ABOUT THE AUTHOR

JEAN CONRAD grew up in the forests of Oregon, where volcanos form a backdrop for an Edenic world of ponderosa pines and white-water streams. She currently lives in New Mexico with her husband.

Conrad is a writer, English teacher at a state university, and part-owner of a Christian bookstore. She also enjoys sketching, playing the piano, gardening, raising canaries, and reading.

Golden Gates is Book 2 in her Windemere Sisters series, a trilogy beginning with *Applegate Landing* and ending with the soon-to-be-published *Rainbow of Promise*.

Forever Classics are inspirational romances designed to bring you a joyful, heart-lifting reading experience. If you would like more information about joining our *Forever Classics* book series, please write to us:

Guideposts Customer Service
39 Seminary Hill Road
Carmel, NY 10512

Forever Classics are chosen by the same staff that prepares *Guideposts*, a monthly magazine filled with true stories of people's adventures in faith. *Guideposts* is not sold on the newsstand. It's available by subscription only. And subscribing is easy. Write to the address above and you can begin reading *Guideposts* soon. When you subscribe, each month you can count on receiving exciting new evidence of God's Presence, His Guidance and His limitless love for all of us.